PiG
AND THE
SHRiNK

YEARLING BOOKS are designed especially to entertain and enlighten young people. Patricia Reilly Giff, consultant to this series, received her bachelor's degree from Marymount College and a master's degree in history from St. John's University. She holds a Professional Diploma in Reading and a Doctorate of Humane Letters from Hofstra University. She was a teacher and reading consultant for many years, and is the author of numerous books for young readers.

pamela todd

PiG
AND THE
SHRiNK

A YEARLING BOOK

Published by
Dell Yearling
an imprint of
Random House Children's Books
a division of Random House, Inc.
1540 Broadway
New York, New York 10036

Visit us on the Web! www.randomhouse.com/kids

Educators and librarians, for a variety of teaching tools, visit us at www.randomhouse.com/teachers

ISBN 0-440-41587-X

Reprinted by arrangement with Delacorte Press

Printed in the United States of America

September 2000

10 9 8 7 6 5 4 3 2 1

OPM

ACKNOWLEDGMENTS

I am grateful to Judy Blume and the Society of Children's Book Writers and Illustrators for awarding this book the society's Work-in-Progress Grant for a Contemporary Novel. Esther Hershenhorn, SCBWI-Illinois, provided me with generous doses of encouragement and support, as she has done for so many writers.

I was greatly helped by those who read this manuscript at various points and gave me valuable insights: Judith Mathews, Carolyn Crimi, Christine Vernon, Lorraine Culver, Hilarie Lieb, Susan Zylstra, the friendly writers of Chautauqua, Nan Morris, Janet Nolan, Judy Dooley, Patti Cone, Betsy Sherman and Delfina Laffler, who planted the seed of our writers' group.

Thanks especially to Pat Allen, Barbara Croft, Joan Fee and Sallie Wolf, four stalwart friends and expert writers who have nurtured this book through many incarnations, and also

Kathy Ryan, my running partner and model of a good therapist,

Richard Drews, who shared his opera stories between carpool stops,

Liz Allen, who embodies Zen and art,

Jo Ellen Siddens, a true steward of nature,

Blanche Gallagher, my soul friend,

Lynn Rogers, whose enthusiasm for children's literature is contagious,

Leslie Wood, who taught me that love knows no language barriers,

and Karen Wojtyla, the editor of my dreams, whose skill, intelligence, and deft touch are apparent throughout.

I am indebted to the parents, teachers and children of Hatch School, past, present and present in spirit; to the people of Grace, who are a daily example to me; and to all those who are part of the great experiment in human compassion that is Oak Park.

First, last and always, thank you to my family: Lynn Gifford and Audrey Warnimont Brown, whose love is a talisman I carry wherever I go; Helen Todd, who's always in there cheering; and my children, Justin, Jessica, Katie and Megan, who are the loves of my life, along with Donn, whom I married for his sense of humor, knowing how much he'd need it.

CHAPTER 1

"Tucker Harrison, report to the principal's office."

I heard the announcement over the laughing and locker slamming, grabbed my binder and my coat and decided to try and make a break for the door.

The last bell of the day had rung and the hall was a river of bumping and jostling people, all flooding toward the exits. I shouldered my way in and let the current carry me along, trying not to be noticed, trying to blend in, as the river rolled past the science lab, down the stairs, through the double doors, then spilled out onto the first floor.

"Steady," I told myself. "Just a few more yards."

The front entrance was directly in front of me now, but I'd have to get past the principal's office to reach it, and Mrs. Fletcher, the school secretary, was talking to someone just inside the door.

There was only one thing to do: crawl. I put my binder in my teeth and dropped to my knees, cautiously picking my way through a forest of moving legs, trying not to get my fingers in the path of someone's Nikes as I made my way toward the light at the end of the hall. I saw the big yellow school bus waiting at the curb, its doors open and beckoning. I saw a pair of red high heels appear out of nowhere, walk toward me and stop directly in front of my face. I saw my life flash before my eyes.

"Almost made it to the getaway bus, didn't you, Tucker?"

Ms. Bodine, the principal, was staring down at me over the tops of her red glasses.

"I was just on my way to see you," I said, taking the binder out of my mouth.

"Really," she said. "I watched you crawl down the entire length of the hallway and I could have sworn you were headed for the door."

"Guess I got turned around," I said weakly.

"Why don't we go to my office together . . . so you won't get lost. It's this way," she said, pointing back down the hall. "And Tucker, this time walk. It's more dignified."

Ms. Bodine was not someone you could easily ignore. She was wearing a flaming red suit, which looked even brighter against her dark brown skin, along with her trademark red high heels and red glasses. She looked like a burning bush. Following her into the office, I couldn't help feeling that the next voice I heard would be the voice of God.

"Sit down, Tucker."

She was staring out the window as she spoke to me, but I could tell she was tense by the way she was clicking her pen.

"I had a talk with Mr. Albert about the handwriting analysis project you came up with for the citywide round of the state science fair. He seems to think you're—"

"Extremely bright, but annoying," I suggested.

"No."

"Just plain annoying?"

"Let me finish, Tucker."

She swung her chair around to look at me across her long gray desk.

"Okay. My lips are zipped," I said, running my thumbnail across them.

"Mr. Albert asked me not to enter your proposal."

"What?" I shouted. "He has no right to do that. He can't!"

"I think your lips came unzipped," she said. "And in any case, I agree with him."

"You what? Oh, I get it, one of those principal-teacher cover-ups."

Ms. Bodine reached into her top drawer, took out a copy of my science fair proposal, flipped through it and slid a page across the desk.

"Read this," she said.

"I don't have to read it. I wrote it."

"I want you to read it out loud. Starting here," she said, pointing to the middle of the page.

"All right," I began softly. " 'The handwriting of Subject

Number One, a middle-school science teacher, is clearly the work of a criminal mind.' "

"Louder, Tucker."

I cleared my throat.

" 'His small capital letters and backward slant indicate an unpredictable personality prone to sudden fits of anger and outbursts of violence, especially toward children. The large down loops show—' "

"That's enough, Tucker. Where did you get all this?"

"I made it up."

She was nodding as though this was exactly the answer she'd expected.

"But I made it up very scientifically. I compared Mr. Albert's handwriting to the handwriting of six guys on death row. They were in a book called *The Science of*—"

"Science?" she interrupted. "This isn't science. It's character assassination."

"But it's all there in black and white," I protested, pointing to the handwriting sample I'd gotten from a detention slip Mr. Albert had written me. "Look at those disgusting *Y* loops and those headless *i*'s and *t*'s. I've never been able to trust anyone who didn't dot their *i*'s and cross their *t*'s, have you?"

Ms. Bodine straightened in her chair.

"I like you, Tucker. I really do. You're a bright, interesting young man. But being smart isn't enough."

She was quiet for a moment.

"We both know how important it is that you do well at the science fair, if you're serious about going to the

State Math and Science Academy next year. Frankly, with the sort of grades you've had the past two years, you're going to need something besides top-notch achievement test scores to get past the admissions committee. That is what you're hoping to do, isn't it, Tucker?" she asked, studying me carefully.

I looked down at my lap and and nodded.

"I'm not going to ban you from participating, but you're going to have to come up with a new proposal," she said.

"It's too late," I protested. "I've already collected handwriting samples from six teachers. I even have one of yours."

"Save them for your memoirs, Tucker. I told Mr. Albert I was willing to take over the role of faculty advisor. I was a science teacher myself before I became a principal, and I thought I might enjoy some hands-on work. Besides, I've always appreciated a challenge."

"I'll make things challenging, Ms. Bodine. You can count on that."

"Yes." She smiled, pressing her fingertips together. "I'm sure you will, Tucker. Even though the science fair isn't until November, I have to have all the paperwork in next week. If you still want to enter it, turn in a new proposal for my approval by Monday morning."

Ms. Bodine slid the rest of my proposal across the desk. There was no budging her. I could see that. The conversation was over. I stuffed the papers into their folder and started to leave.

"One more thing," she called out to me. I turned to face

her again. "Always remember that science is a tool for helping people, Tucker."

I went out into the empty hallway with those words echoing in my head: "Science is a tool for helping people."

But who could I help when there was so little time?

CHAPTER 2

One of the things that gets me into trouble a lot is that I have the kind of mind that can't sit still. After supper that evening I went up to my room, sat down at the computer and told myself I'd stay there, glued to the chair, until I'd come up with a winner of a science fair project.

My mind had other ideas.

"Why don't you go look out the window?" it suggested slyly. "I think someone's trying to break into the house. Hey, wait, isn't this the day *Real Emergency* is on TV, or was it Thursday? Better go get the *TV Guide* after you check to make sure everything's safe. And since you'll be going past the kitchen anyway, pick up some pretzels and a Coke."

I cut the words THINK SCIENCE out of red construction paper and tacked them over the *Titanic* poster on the wall behind my desk. But I couldn't think of science without imagining Ms. Bodine standing in the doorway of my room, looking even larger and redder than she does in real life.

By the time our housekeeper, Mrs. Hrabik, came upstairs at ten o'clock, all I had printed out was one sheet of paper with the title "101 Ways to Use Science to Save Humanity," followed by 101 blank spaces.

"Mrs. boy sleep now," she said, drying her hands on her apron. She always called my mother "Mrs." and me "Mrs. boy," no matter how many times I told her she could call me Tucker.

"Too much work make head ick," she said, tapping her head.

"Head *ache,* Mrs. Hrabik. Too much work makes your head ache."

"Ahhhhh," she said, breaking into a big smile. "Smart boy. Good head."

I turned off the lights and the computer, and Mrs. Hrabik went back downstairs. When I heard the television, I got up and turned the computer back on again and sat there in the dark.

It felt good to be alone, with only the blue light of my computer glowing all around me. I twirled my chair and watched the numbers projected on my wall by the digital clock slowly changing: 11:08 . . . 11:09. I switched the computer to the outer space screen saver, then tilted my chair back and looked up at the glow-in-the-dark galaxy on my bedroom ceiling. All those stars. All those planets. All that empty space.

If only it were real, I thought. If only I could sail out into space and find a black hole to fall into. Maybe I'd land in a parallel universe where there were no science fairs and schools were strictly prohibited by law; where people had computer chips instead of brains and you didn't have to learn things, you just loaded them.

I must have been sitting there for at least an hour when I heard someone come in, climb the stairs and knock on my door.

"Still awake?"

My mom leaned into my room, yawning, wearing the bright blue suit she'd had on when she left for the conference that morning. When she was home she usually wore jeans, and she was so small that you could mistake her for a kid. But when she went to work, she put a lot of effort into looking good.

"It's after midnight, Tucker. Mrs. Hrabik told me you went to sleep hours ago."

"I know. I had some homework to finish up."

"What are you doing on the computer?" she asked, peering over my shoulder.

"Looking for the Escape key."

I hit "Esc" and the screen went blue again.

"Whew," I said. "Now I can finally go to sleep."

I went over and flopped down on my bed. My mom sat down next to me and kissed me on the top of the head. She smelled like the eucalyptus leaves she kept on her desk because they were supposed to make you feel calmer.

"And just what were you trying to escape from?" she said softly.

"The screen saver," I said. "It was trying to suck me in. I think computers are scary, don't you?"

"Not as scary as boys your age who stay up until midnight."

She leaned her head forward and rubbed the back of her neck.

"What an ultramarathon day," she said. "How was yours? School go okay?"

"Mmm," I said, relieved that it was too dark for her to see my face clearly. "How was your speech?"

"Great. They loved it. The chairman asked me if I could present it at the meeting of the American Psychological Association next spring."

"Wow."

"Now get some rest," she said, unclipping an earring as she walked to the door. "You'll do better when you're fresh. Take it from a fellow drudge."

I watched the numbers on the wall change for a long time after the house was quiet. When I finally did doze off, I dreamt that I was sitting in a dark cell, waiting to see if the governor would pardon me for not turning in my science fair project on time. Ms. Bodine walked in, dressed in a gray prison guard's uniform, only with red high heels.

"We just had word from the governor," she said, and she gave me both thumbs down. "Would you prefer death by hanging or electric chair?"

"How about poison?" I suggested.

"Sorry," she said, "the cafeteria's closed."

Then she threw her head back and laughed a horrible evil laugh that echoed up and down the hall.

* * *

I managed to waste the rest of the weekend in my room, peering into the microscope, flipping through books on fossils, staring out the window through my telescope, and doing other scientific things to convince myself that I was actually working, even though I was getting nowhere.

Monday morning, I still had no project. I stumbled downstairs wondering what I could tell Ms. Bodine to stall her. My mom stood at the stove, wearing her white terry-cloth robe and the matching slippers that flapped when she walked. She was cooking an omelette, but she stopped and studied my face.

"Is something wrong, Tucker?" she asked.

I hate when she does that. It makes me feel like my brain is naked and everything I think about is spelled out in red letters flashing across my forehead. It's like that sign at the bank that says, "See us about low-interest loans . . . First National Bank." Only my brain was spelling out, "I'm in deep trouble. Ask me what I've done wrong."

"Yes," I said. "But I don't have time to talk about it right now."

My mom's a therapist, so I didn't bother lying to her. She says it's her business to know when people are lying and to try to help them tell the truth—especially to themselves.

"Okay," she said, with only a shadow of concern darkening her face. "If you change your mind, I'm here. By the way, I should be home early tonight. My five o'clock appointment canceled. Maybe we could go to the Hunan Palace for dinner and talk."

"Great," I said flatly. "I mean, great. That's great!"

I took a box of breakfast bars out of the cabinet, shoved one in my backpack, grabbed my coat and headed for the door.

"Hey. What about the omelette?"

"Can't. I'm late for the bus."

"Oh, I almost forgot," Mom yelled after me. "Your dad called and wanted me to tell you he'll be in town for a meeting in two weeks. He wants to see you, Tucker. He asked about your science fair project."

That's nice, I thought. Now I can give him the news of my utter and complete failure in person.

As I walked down the sidewalk, I saw the yellow school bus parked at my stop and I broke into a run.

"Wait," I yelled, but the driver didn't hear. I watched the bus pull away and saw Jonah Roegel and some of his friends in the window laughing. Jonah yanked the window open and stuck his arm out to wave good-bye.

It was beginning to feel like my whole life was one big struggle to catch up and I was falling farther and farther behind.

Ms. Bodine was wrong about one thing. It wasn't the idea of not making it into the State Math and Science

Academy that bothered me. It was the thought of explaining it to my dad.

My dad is a neurosurgeon. He lives in Boston now that he and my mother are divorced and he's remarried, so I don't get to see him very often. But he calls me a lot, and every Wednesday he dictates a letter, mostly full of advice about working hard and making something out of myself. The mailman must think I'm dying of some awful disease because every letter I get says Boston General Hospital on the outside.

My father decided a long time ago that I was going to be a scientist like him, and he's spent a lot of time and money getting me ready for it. He gives me microscopes and chemistry sets, buys me subscriptions to science magazines and even sends me on science vacations. I'm probably the only kid in my school who has been to computer camp, space camp, dinosaur camp and spelunking camp. My mother says he's giving me the childhood he wanted but never got. Most of the time, I'd be glad to let him have it for himself.

I suppose I could have gone back inside and asked my mom for a ride, but I knew she'd ask more questions than I had answers for, and there were enough grown-ups in my life doing that already. Besides, if I walked, I would have more time to try and think up a science project that would make Ms. Bodine happy. All I had to do was find someone to help.

It was a warm October day, and the streets were full of people walking, working and waiting for buses. I studied each one I passed to see if they had some kind of problem that science could help them solve. A few blocks from my house I noticed a truck parked outside a red-brick house. In the doorway there were two men lugging an enormous piano down a flight of steps. Now, there were guys who needed help. I pulled my notebook and pen out of my backpack and scribbled, "Idea #1: Disposable piano." Bet there'd be a market for that one. I could think of more than a few kids who'd like to dispose of their pianos.

Down the street I came across a billboard of a woman bent over a child in a stroller. She was wiping up several brown streams of chocolate ice cream that had dribbled down his face, his hands and his shirt. "Idea #2," I wrote quickly in my notebook. "Dripless ice cream." I walked several more blocks, turning over all the possibilities. Use dry milk? Insulate the cone?

Just before I reached the school, I went past a man pulling weeds in dirty blue jeans and a baseball cap. "Idea #3: Self-weeding plants," I wrote, and closed the notebook to think about how I could do it. Maybe I could develop a vegetarian Venus flytrap that would eat its neighbors, then cross it with a carrot.

It was beginning to sound promising until a headline suddenly flashed through my mind. "Killer Carrots Take Over Town. Governor Puts National Guard on Alert. Police Looking for Mysterious Science Boy."

Who was I trying to fool? It was hopeless. Ms. Bodine had given me a whole weekend to figure out a new science fair project, and the best I could come up with was a plan for ecological disaster. The only sensible thing to do was give up and withdraw from the competition.

I walked into school late, went to my locker to put away my books and coat, and was going to go straight to Ms. Bodine's office to tell her my career as a scientist was over. But that was when I ran into Pig.

CHAPTER 3

Angelo Pighetti was the kid in our class who was always picked on because he was fat. Everyone in school knew that Pig weighed exactly 180 pounds, just like everyone knew that I was 4 feet, 10 inches tall. Mrs. Schroenhamer, the school nurse, shouted it across the gym every spring when she weighed and measured us. I'm sure Mrs. Schroenhamer had never actually been a kid herself, or she would have known better than to announce our heights and weights to the whole gym class.

I was standing by my locker when Pig came out of nowhere and crashed into me.

"Sorry," he panted, picking me up off the floor. He bent over and picked up the brown paper bag he had dropped and shoved it into my chest.

"Take this, would you?"

"What is it?"

"It's my lunch."

"No thanks," I said, shoving it back at him. "I already have one."

"I don't want you to eat it," he said, thrusting it at me again. "I just want you to put it somewhere for a while."

I was going to ask him why, but I was interrupted.

"Here, piggy, piggy," someone called from around the corner.

"It's Jonah," he whispered. "He's going to cream me."

"If I were you I'd run for it," I urged him.

"I can't," Pig said, his eyes darting back down the hall. "He'll catch me . . . and he's got two friends with him."

"In that case, you'd better hide."

Pig looked at me, then down the hall again.

"You're right," he said.

Pig tossed his lunch into my locker, then tried to squeeze in after it.

"You're not getting away, Pighetti," Jonah called out, his voice getting closer.

"Give me a push," Pig said.

"It's not going to work. You'd better get out of here, fast."

"I can't," said Pig, twisting up his face. "I'm stuck."

I closed the locker door as far as I could and threw my coat over the part of Pig that was sticking out. Then I walked to the end of the hall to head them off.

Jonah and his friends smirked as they came toward me.

"Well, if it isn't the incredible shrinking boy," Jonah sneered. "Where's Pig, Shrinko?"

"I haven't seen him for a while," I said, moving my body to try and block Jonah's view of the other hall.

"You know, I find that a little hard to believe," he said, stepping closer and talking down into my face. He was at least a head taller than me, and he seemed to grow several inches when he was mad. "I just saw him come this way, and he's got my lunch. I'm going to be awfully hungry today if I don't find him. And when I get hungry, I get mean."

"You must be hungry a lot," I said.

"You're very funny, Harrison. I'm laughing so hard it hurts. Like you're going to feel unless you tell me which way he went."

He took my backpack, reached in and pulled out the breakfast bar. I tried to grab it away from him, but he shoved me backward into the lockers.

Jonah unwrapped the breakfast bar, chomped on it, then screwed up his face.

"Yeech, apricot," he said, opening up my backpack and spitting it back in. "You must be missing some taste buds."

He unzipped the pockets and looked inside while his friends snickered with appreciation.

"Didn't your mommy give you any cash in case you have to call home?"

Jonah handed my backpack to one of his friends, who threw it over his shoulder. It hit the wall with a thud.

"Look, I don't know where Pig is and I don't have anything you want," I said.

"You've got that right." Jonah laughed. "What you've got, we don't want. If you see Pig, tell him his friend Jonah is looking for him. Later, Shrink."

18

He mussed up my hair and shoved me out of the way as he and his friends walked off, laughing. I waited until they were gone, then walked back to my locker.

"Boy, I hate that kid," I said, opening up my backpack to check the damage and finding the wad of chewed breakfast bar stuck to my science book.

Pig knocked the coat off onto the floor and whistled with relief.

"That was close. If he'd found me I'd be trying to squeeze into my coffin. Help me out of here, okay?"

"Only if you tell me why you took his lunch and why you threw it in *my* locker. Are you trying to get me killed or something?"

"I didn't take his lunch," Pig said indignantly. "It's my lunch. He steals it every day. And when he's really in a good mood, he gives me his, which is always salami and mustard on stale bread. Now, would you help me out?"

I put my foot on the locker and pulled hard on his arm.

"Why does he always steal *your* lunch?" I asked, straining.

"I . . . guess . . . it's . . . because I'm—" Pig grunted through clenched teeth.

"Suck in your gut," I interrupted him.

". . . sort of . . ."

Suddenly Pig came loose and we both flew across the hall, crashing into the lockers on the other side.

". . . a gourmet," he finished.

I picked myself up off the floor and dusted the dirt off the back of my pants as Pig went to pick up my scattered books.

"Why don't you just quit bringing such good lunches to school?" I asked.

"I already tried that," Pig said, dumping the pile of books in my arms. "He beat me up because he said I was a bad cook . . . which shows how much he knows. I even tried not bringing any lunch at all for one whole week so there wouldn't be anything for him to steal."

"So, what happened?"

Pig's big dark eyebrows flew up and he threw his hands in the air.

"He still beat me up. He told me he liked punching fat kids because it didn't hurt his hands."

I shook my head.

"And I thought being short was hard."

"Yeah, well, being fat's harder, especially if you're a good cook. I gotta go," Pig said, slinging his backpack over his shoulder. "This is the third time I've been late this week."

"Hey, can I ask you something?" I said. "Why do you let everyone call you Pig?"

Pig shrugged. "Do you really think it would be easier if I made them call me Angelo?"

"I see your point."

He started off down the hall, then turned back.

"Thanks, Tucker," he said. "I won't forget this."

I walked over to close my locker, counting up my gains and losses. I had disappointed the principal, failed my father and made enemies out of the three meanest kids in school. Not a bad morning's work, even for me. On the

20

other hand, Pig hadn't got beaten up and neither had I . . . at least not yet. And Pig still had his lunch. But when I went to close my locker, I found Pig's brown paper bag still sitting inside. If I could just get it back to him by lunchtime without running into Jonah . . .

CHAPTER 4

Once in a while you do something that's hard to take back. You knock over the first domino and the rest just keep falling. When I walked into Ms. Bodine's office that morning, I had a bad feeling that no matter what I did, the next sound I heard would be the *click, click* of my dominoes as they all came crashing down.

"Tucker," she said, looking surprisingly glad to see me. "It seems I owe you an apology."

"You do?" I said.

She leaned back in her chair and adjusted the red and black scarf that was draped over her shoulders.

"Yes," she said. "I do. I underestimated you, Tucker. I was afraid your back was up against the wall and you were going to decide not to enter the science fair at all. I didn't really expect you to have a new idea for your project, but here you are, first thing in the morning. You're a lot more persistent than I gave you credit for. So, tell me. What did you come up with?"

I sat down in the chair across from her. Ms. Bodine was staring intently at me behind those bright red glasses and rocking slowly back and forth. I was going to say that I hadn't come up with anything, that I was not the science wizard everyone wanted me to be. I just kept staring into those red-rimmed lenses, thinking about my father and listening to the squeak of the chair as she rocked back and forth, back and forth. My mouth felt like it was paralyzed, and when it finally started to move, something horrible came out.

"I've come up with a fantastic science project," I said. It sounded like my voice was coming from a long way away, as though it had grown tired of taking orders from my brain and decided to strike out on its own.

There was total silence in her office as we both waited to hear what I would say next.

"It's . . . s-s-something . . . that will help p-people," I stammered.

Ms. Bodine leaned forward. She stared over the top of her glasses as though she could get a clearer picture of things that way.

"Could you be a little more . . . specific?" she asked.

I was nervously fingering Pig's brown paper lunch bag, which I'd been carrying with me for safekeeping. I coughed out the first word that came into my head.

"Food," I said.

There was a painfully long pause.

"Right," I said, nodding. "It has to do with food."

After all, what could be more helpful than food?

"You mean," she said, cocking her head, "nutrition?"

"Right, nutrition."

"And . . . ?" she said.

"And what?" I asked.

"Tucker, are we playing Twenty Questions here? Because I don't have time right now for games."

Ms. Bodine took off her glasses, set them down on her desk and rested her face in both hands. She sighed and shook her head.

"I'm not sure I know exactly what you mean when you say you want to do a science fair project on nutrition. Nutrition and what?"

I was frantically trying to remember everything I had seen, heard or thought about science in the last twenty-four hours. When I rifled through the images in my head, all I could find was a picture of Pig rushing down the hall and slamming into me.

"Fat kids," I blurted out.

She stared at me as though I had just said something shocking.

"Food . . . and . . . fat kids," she said, drawing each word out of her mouth like caramels stuck to her teeth. Then her face suddenly cleared and she leaned back in her chair.

"Oooooh. I think I see," she said, wiping her glasses and putting them back on again. "Your project is on nutrition and obesity. Yes. I can see the potential for a good project there."

"You can?" I said. "I mean . . . that's good. I can too."

"The surgeon general has made obesity his new cam-

24

paign. I was reading about it in the newspaper just the other day."

She reached in her drawer, pulled out a yellow lined tablet of paper and started jotting down some notes.

"Now, tell me, what exactly are you going to do?"

"What exactly am I going to do? What exactly am I going to do?" I repeated like one of those toy parrots that have tape recorders in place of brains.

Luckily, the secretary came in.

"I'm sorry to interrupt you, Ms. Bodine, but Dr. Levinson asked me if he could see you for a few minutes."

Ms. Bodine sighed. "Well, I guess we'll have to finish this later, Tucker. Your idea sounds good. Why don't you go ahead and write it up and turn it in to me by Friday?"

She stood up and walked me to the door with her arm around my shoulder.

"I'm really very proud of you, Tucker," she said.

Well, I thought, there goes the last domino. *Click, click, click, click, thud.*

CHAPTER 5

I went through the rest of the morning in a daze. My body may have been walking down hallways and sitting in classes, but my head was on temporary assignment elsewhere. Food, fat kids. I knew I could find lots of theories about why kids get fat, but I couldn't just write up everyone else's ideas for the science fair. I needed some kind of experiment.

I was relieved when the bell finally rang for lunch and I hurried to the lunchroom, hoping to get there before Jonah. I picked out a table in a corner where I could be alone and set Pig's lunch down in front of me. It was the first time I had paid any attention to it, even though I'd been carrying it around all morning. It was in a bulging brown paper bag that was twisted shut at the top with grease soaking through on the outside. When I'd sat down in Spanish class earlier, two girls sitting next to me got up to move, and now I knew why. My fingers reeked of garlic just from carrying it around. I started to untwist the top, carefully, as though whatever was inside might jump out at me, when something made the table jerk.

It was Pig.

"Hi, Tucker," he said, flopping down in the seat across from me. "Okay if I sit here?"

"Well . . . actually . . . I have some thinking to do for my science fair project."

"You're not supposed to think on your lunch hour. Your brain will overheat," he said, fanning his head with both hands. "Hey, great, you brought my food."

He reached over and pulled the bag to his side of the table and pulled out a large slice of cold pizza.

"Want some?" he asked, tearing the piece in two and putting half on a napkin for me.

He took a big bite out of his piece. There was something slimy and brown hanging from his lower lip and he sucked it into his mouth.

"I love anchovies," he said. "They remind me of worms."

He looked down at the untouched piece on my napkin.

"What's the matter? You don't like them?"

I made a face as he reached for my half of the pizza.

"Want me to take 'em off?"

"That's okay," I said. "Why don't you just eat the whole piece?"

"Great, then you can have the pepperoni," he said, pulling out another piece.

I shook my head.

"Green pepper and onion?" he asked, putting his hand in the bag again.

"What is this, Domino's Mobile Unit?" I asked.

"I know what you'd like," Pig said. "Sausage. Everybody likes sausage."

I held up my half-eaten turkey sandwich. "Thanks, but this is enough."

Pig finished off the pizza, then reached in and pulled out a package of Twinkies, opened it and took a bite. "I hate it when that happens," he said.

"What?"

"When you take a bite and don't get any cream with the cake. Wouldn't you think they'd put the cream all the way to the end?"

"Look, it's really hard for me to concentrate like this," I said.

"Maybe I can help you with your science fair project," Pig said agreeably. "Two heads are better than one. As a matter of fact, two of anything is better than one."

He finished off the first package of Twinkies and started to rip open a second.

"I don't believe this," I said.

"Oh, sorry," he said, holding out the half-open package. "You want some?"

"Haven't you ever heard the expression 'You are what you eat'?"

"Yeah," Pig said, chuckling to himself. "I guess that makes me a Twinkie."

He licked the cream off his fingers one at a time.

"I could do worse," he said, shrugging. "I could be like Jonah. He must eat snake meat. Rattlesnake meat."

28

"Nah, rattlesnakes aren't mean enough," I said. "He'd have to eat some large, vicious and cunning predator. You know, like a man. You don't suppose he eats people, do you?"

"He would if they were prepared properly." He chuckled.

Pig had a round face with huge twinkly dark eyes, and his whole body shook when he laughed. I found myself liking him just for the way he laughed.

He leaned across the table toward me. "You know where he went to school before he transferred here this fall?" he asked in a hushed voice. I shook my head.

"Gordon, that school they only lock you up in if you do something really bad, like kill your dog or something. Even the warden was afraid of him. They had to slide his food under the bars with a stick."

I raised my eyebrows and blinked at him. "Gordon's not a jail. It's a reform school. They don't keep kids in cells. Where did you get all this?"

"Beth Ellen Hertzel," he said.

"How can you trust anyone who wears black lipstick?"

Pig looked around at the tables near us to see if anyone was listening.

"She's psychic," he whispered.

"You mean psych-o, not -ic," I said.

"You wouldn't be laughing if you knew the whole story," Pig said. "Her aunt works there. She's a guard."

I rolled my eyes up to the ceiling. "They don't have guards, they have teachers. And if any relatives of Beth

29

Ellen's are at Gordon, it's not because they're employees. Besides, if he was as bad as you say, why would they turn him loose?"

Pig put the last piece of Twinkie in his mouth.

"I don't know. Maybe he was a bad influence on the other prisoners. He was probably trying to organize a prison riot so they expelled him. Or maybe he was teaching the new guys how to beat people up and steal their food."

The bell rang and there was a great deal of shouting and scraping of chairs as the crowd in the lunchroom got up to leave for class. Pig wadded up his brown paper bag and I gathered up my books, tossing my mostly uneaten sandwich into the garbage can as I left.

"Maybe we could have lunch together tomorrow," Pig said as we walked into the hallway together. "I thought you were kind of a . . . you know, a science nerd . . . because I heard you were all keyed up about winning the science fair. But actually, you're a lot like me."

"Thanks . . . I guess."

"And I meant what I said this morning. If you ever need help—"

"Wait a minute," I said, grabbing hold of his arm. Science fair, fat people, find someone to help. Suddenly everything was coming together. I turned and looked directly into Angelo Pighetti's dark eyes.

"Do you really want to help me?"

"Sure," he said, shrugging.

I took a deep breath and jumped right in.

"I want you to be my science fair project," I said.

He looked at me, confused.

"It's on food and fat kids. I want to prove I know what I'm talking about by helping someone lose weight."

Pig yanked his arm away. "I don't want to be anyone's science fair project . . . and I don't want to lose weight. I like me the way I am."

"I do too. But you are a little . . . overweight," I said, fumbling for the right word.

"So what? Some of the greatest people in history have been fat. Look at Winston Churchill. Look at Santa Claus. Look at . . . Cupid."

"It wasn't being fat that made them great. Couldn't you be like them and be thin?"

"Not if it means I have to quit eating. I like eating. I like cooking." He rubbed his chin and thought about it a minute; then he shrugged. "I like everything about food."

"You don't have to give up food altogether."

"So what do you want me to do? Have one of those fat-sucking operations where they vacuum it all away?"

He made a sucking noise and pretended there was a vacuum cleaner stuck to his thigh. I shook my head.

"All you need is someone like me to teach you how to eat."

"I *know* how to eat, Tucker."

He glanced down the hallway, which was beginning to empty out.

"Yeah. You're an Einstein at it. But I could teach you how to eat healthy foods . . . low-fat, whole grains, the sort of thing your mom always wants you to eat. You'll be helping yourself as much as you're helping me."

"No thanks, Tucker."

"But think of all the advantages of being thin. You could run faster and move around easier. You could fit in lockers better."

"I've gotta go," Pig said, starting off down the hall.

"Wait! What about Jonah and those other kids who tease you? Do you want to spend the rest of your life trying to get away from them?"

Pig wheeled around and faced me.

"Jonah thinks he can beat me up and steal my lunch every day just because I'm fat, and you think *I'm* the one with the problem," he said, poking me in the chest. "Don't you get it? Jonah doesn't beat me up because I'm fat. He beats me up because he enjoys it. Being mean is his hobby."

Pig tilted his head and stuck his lips out. "So the answer is still no, okay?"

"If you don't want to do it for yourself, do it for all the other fat kids you'll be helping by being part of my experiment." I said. "It's kind of like donating your body to science, only you don't have to die first."

"I might as well be dead if I have to eat the stuff you want me to eat. Find yourself another science fair project, Tucker."

Pig turned and walked away, but I jumped ahead, facing him.

"I don't *have* another science project. Just lose some weight for the science fair, and then if you don't like it, I'll take you out right after the award ceremonies and you can have a Twinkie pizza if you want. Have ten of them. My treat."

The bell rang for the next class. We were already late. Pig started to walk around me, but I stepped in front of him.

"Wait."

I stared at the floor.

"I wouldn't ask you to do this if I wasn't desperate. I promised my dad I'd come up with something really good for the science fair so I can get in the Math and Science Academy. It's the last chance I have, and I can't let him down again."

Pig was silent for a long time.

"Please, Pig."

He stared down the empty corridor. There was the sound of someone opening a door somewhere and slamming it shut again.

"Okay, okay," he said with a long sigh. "I'll do it. But I don't think I'm going to like this."

CHAPTER 6

There were two reasons I was glad my mom and I were going out to dinner that night. One was that now that I'd convinced Pig to lose weight, I had to figure out how I was going to help him do it. My mom might come in handy there. After all, she was a shrink. She ought to know something about fat kids.

The other reason was that the Hunan Palace was one of my favorite places to eat. It was dark as a cave, with red carpets and red walls covered with pictures of dragons. The only light came from red and yellow Chinese lanterns that hung down low over the booths.

The dining room was guarded by a bigger-than-life-size statue of a Chinese warrior with fierce eyes and a mustache that drooped down to his chin. He held a sword straight out in front of him and his arm was hinged. You had to lift it up to walk in.

But the best thing about the Hunan Palace was the owner, Mr. Wong. We ate there at least once a week, and he always treated us like we were friends instead of just customers he had to be nice to so he would get a big tip.

"Mrs. Harrison, Tucker, come in, come in," he said, reaching for two menus as we arrived.

"Right this way. I saved your favorite table," he said. Then he leaned down and covered his mouth with one hand.

"A fortune cookie told me you'd be coming in," he whispered in my ear.

"Sure," I said, and pretended to crack open a cookie and unroll the fortune. "Fire up the wok. The Harrisons are coming."

"Oh no, fortune cookies never name names," Mr. Wong protested. "It said, 'Good luck is headed your way.' It's all in the interpretation, Tucker, all in the interpretation."

He gave us a minute to browse through the menu after we sat down, then returned to our table.

"What would you like tonight, Mrs. Harrison?"

"I think I'll have the hot and spicy chicken, Mr. Wong. Make it industrial strength. I need something that will make me wake up and pay attention tonight. Throw caution to the wind. Don't spare the chili peppers," she said, flipping her dark hair back out of her eyes and flinging her arms wide.

"Don't worry, Mrs. Harrison. No one has ever fallen asleep over a bowl of Mr. Wong's hot and spicy chicken. What about you, Tucker?"

"The usual, Mr. Wong. One McHunan burger with cheese, hold the pickles, hold the lettuce, American orders don't upset us. Don't forget, no MSG."

Mr. Wong shook his head.

"You American children. No wonder you're always bored. No sense of adventure. No daring. No risk. One day I will convince you to try real food. Then you will see. It will make your toes curl and smoke come out of your nose."

He made a ferocious face, and in the dim light I could almost imagine wisps of white smoke curling up from his nostrils.

"You see that dragon up there?" he asked, pointing to a picture on the wall of a red and yellow beast with flames leaping from its open mouth. "One of Mr. Wong's happy customers," he said; then he leaned in close to me. "It could be you, Tucker."

I thought about how I had told Pig you are what you eat. For a second I thought I saw my face in the picture instead of the dragon's, with a tiny Jonah trapped beneath my claws. My mom waved a hand in front of my face to break my stare.

"Enough," she said, laughing. "Don't encourage him, Mr. Wong. One fire breather in the family is plenty."

Mr. Wong disappeared into the kitchen, and Mom poured tea into two small white china cups while I tried to figure out a way to bring up the subject of Pig without going into a long and possibly unpleasant explanation of my science fair project. I decided to try and ease into the subject gradually.

"So . . . Mom," I said, "have you seen any fat clients lately?"

"What did you say?"

She set down the teapot with a loud *clunk*. I could see this wasn't going to be easy.

"I was just wondering if you knew anything about helping people who are overweight."

She fingered her favorite yin-yang pendant, which hung down the front of her black turtleneck, and studied me carefully.

"Well, I usually don't see clients for that reason alone. May I ask what brought this up?"

I took a deep breath.

"I had to dream up a new science fair project. Ms. Bodine didn't think my first one was good enough, so I decided to study fat kids instead."

"Oh!" she said, her eyes widening.

"What does make kids fat?" I asked.

She shrugged.

"Lots of different things. It could be metabolism . . . or genetics. Kids with overweight parents are more likely to be overweight themselves. Lack of exercise and poor nutrition can certainly play a part. But often it's just a stage the child will outgrow."

"What if you wanted to help someone outgrow it, faster I mean, like in a couple of weeks?"

"There are no quick fixes. Most kids just need to concentrate on good health habits, and eventually things fall into place."

She took a sip of tea and cocked her head a little. I must have accidentally set off her mom alarm.

"Tucker, is there something going on here you're not telling me about?"

"What makes you think that?"

She stared up at the Chinese lantern for a minute, thinking, and then she looked back at me. My mom has big green eyes and she draws dark lines around them to make them look even bigger. When she stares at you, it feels like she's looking right into your brain.

"It's just a feeling I have . . . that something's worrying you. I know we haven't had much time together lately, but I'm always here if you need to talk."

"Everything's fine," I said. "I'm just a little nervous about my science fair project."

There was a high-pitched beeping sound from her briefcase. She dug into it and pulled her pager out.

"Uh-oh," she said, pressing the button and reading the numbers off the top. "This is one I have to return. Excuse me a minute."

She slid out of the booth just as Mr. Wong appeared with a tray of food.

"Mrs. Harrison," he said, setting down a plate of steaming chicken chunks smothered with red and green chili peppers. "You're not losing courage, are you?"

"I just have to make a phone call, then I'll be back." She laughed. "Your chicken doesn't scare me."

She walked toward the back where the phones were and Mr. Wong put the cheeseburger and a bowl of rice down in front of me.

"A steady, reliable and hardworking woman, your mother," said Mr. Wong, pouring me another cup of tea. "She is an ox, is she not?" Mr. Wong was smiling kindly at me, as though he had just paid my mother a great compliment.

"My mom? An ox? I don't think I'd say that exactly. At least not to her face."

He laughed out loud and his hand jiggled, almost spilling the tea.

"Oh no, Tucker, you misunderstand. I do not mean to give offense. I was only guessing that she must have been born in the year of the ox."

I stared blankly at him.

"The Chinese zodiac," he said. Mr. Wong could see he wasn't getting through to me. He sat down in the booth across from me and poured himself a cup of tea. Then he leaned forward, the Chinese lantern above his head giving his face a strange pattern of light and shadow.

"In the Chinese calendar, each year is associated with one of twelve animals, and children born during that year are believed to have the characteristics of that animal. It is somewhat like your Western horoscopes. Women born in the year of the ox are honest, patient and strong. No-nonsense people, you would call them."

"How can you know what people are like by knowing the year they were born? It doesn't sound very scientific."

Mr. Wong shrugged. He stared past me as he spoke. "Who can say? I can only tell you that my grandfather lived by the zodiac, and he died a happy old man, with much wealth and many children who honored him. You see, Chinese astrologers also believe that you can

39

achieve success and happiness with the help of the zo-diac."

Mr. Wong leaned closer to me. "If you want to make wise choices, you must consult the will of natural forces."

"What animal would I be?" I asked.

"Let me see," Mr. Wong said, laying a finger on his chin. "You are in what grade?"

"Seventh," I said.

"Then I would guess you will turn thirteen sometime after February."

"How did you know that?"

Mr. Wong smiled.

"You are a rat, Tucker."

"Gee, thanks."

"No, no. This is an honor. Rats are much-maligned creatures, but they have many good qualities. They are inventive, determined and resourceful, with a quick sense of humor. I think that describes you very well, don't you?" he asked, smiling and putting his hand on my shoulder.

My mother returned to the table and Mr. Wong stood up.

"Tucker, I'm afraid we're going to have to leave," she said. "I've got a problem with a patient that really can't wait. Mr. Wong, would you mind wrapping up our dinners so we can take them with us?"

"Certainly, Mrs. Harrison," he said, bowing his head slightly.

Mr. Wong took our food to the kitchen and Mom reached over to give me a hug.

"I'm sorry, Tucker. I guess we'll have to continue this conversation later. I want to know more about your science project. It sounds interesting."

"That's all?" I asked, disappointed. "Just interesting? I'm not going to win with interesting. I need astonishing."

She smiled warmly. "Whatever you do, I'm sure it will take the judge's breath away."

Mr. Wong came back and handed my mother a brown paper shopping bag. "A pleasant evening to you, Mrs. Harrison."

"Thank you, Mr. Wong." She walked over to get her coat and I hung back to ask one last question.

"Can the zodiac tell me how my science fair project is going to turn out?"

Mr. Wong smiled. "The future is in your own hands, Tucker. But I *can* tell you that it is an auspicious time for you. It is a good year for the children of the rat, a year that will bring great triumph, but only to those rats who work for the benefit of others."

My mom handed me my coat and slipped her jacket over her shoulders.

"By the way, what year is this?" I asked.

"It is the year of the boar," Mr. Wong said.

"Boar? Isn't that . . . a wild pig?"

"Precisely, Tucker."

"The year of the Pig," I murmured slowly, letting the thought work its way into the corners of my mind.

41

"I have to know more about this," I said suddenly.

There was a trace of a smile on Mr. Wong's face. "Of course, Tucker."

"But I'm afraid it will have to wait," my mom interrupted, touching my arm lightly. "We really must be going."

I wanted to keep the conversation going, but I knew there was no use trying to talk my mom into staying when one of her patients needed her.

"Good-bye, Mr. Wong," I said. "Maybe we'll be back later in the week."

"I would be honored by your visit," he said, bowing slightly. Then he opened the door for us and we stepped out into the night.

CHAPTER 7

I told Pig I'd meet with him on Wednesday and spent the next day doing research at the library and on the Internet. By the time I was done, I had a stack of books and articles and a lot of information written down in my notebook under the heading "Fascinating Facts About Fat." It turned out that a lot of people besides me and the surgeon general were interested in the topic, because the problem of obesity was growing in more ways than one. The number of overweight kids had more than doubled in the last thirty years.

I also found out my mom had been right. Most everyone seemed to agree the solution wasn't drastic dieting. It was getting kids to eat low-fat, high-nutrition foods and get lots of exercise. So long, Cocoa Puffs in front of the television—hello, celery sticks by the pool.

When my alarm went off Wednesday morning, I stayed in bed a few extra minutes to enjoy the feeling I had that everything was going to be all right. Nutrition and obesity. Just saying the words made me feel like a scientist. They were the kind of words my father liked, the kind with lots of syllables. And now I had the experiment I needed too. Maybe, just maybe, I could make this work. It was all a matter of teaching Pig what to eat and getting him to eat it. How hard could that possibly be?

I wanted the Pig Project to be my secret weapon, so I decided to say as little as possible about it. That way, I could surprise everyone on the day of the science fair with my amazing experiment on a real live fat kid.

I closed my eyes and imagined myself standing at the front of an auditorium packed with principals, teachers, scientists and government officials. I'd be at the podium, surrounded by TV cameras and reporters holding microphones in my face, and behind me there would be a gigantic blowup of Angelo Pighetti when he was fat. Standing next to me would be the real Angelo Pighetti, now amazingly slim, covered with a sheet. I'd give my report on nutrition; then for the grand finale, I'd pull off the sheet and everyone would see Pig and gasp. Pig would tell the audience how much better his life was without those extra pounds. Then the mayor would leap onto the stage to award me the first-place ribbon.

Cameras would flash and reporters would elbow each other to get close enough to ask questions as I left the stage. "Amazing Science Boy Discovers Cure for Fat," the newspaper articles would read, and underneath that there'd be a smaller headline: "Boy Wonder Opens Chain of Weight Loss Clinics (see Business Section)." It was the year of the Pig, a good time for new ventures, and it was beginning to seem like I was going to enjoy being a scientist after all.

The rest of that day went by quickly. I hardly even noticed that I was in school until the bell rang at the end and it was time to leave. I had called Pig the night before and asked him to meet me at the back entrance so we could walk to my house. When I got there, he was by the athletic field, leaning on the fence, watching the soccer team practice. It was one of those days that made your cheeks sting and your fingers numb. Pig was wearing a black Sox cap, baggy jeans, sneakers with the laces hanging loose and an open jacket with a black Michael Jordan T-shirt underneath.

I tapped his shoulder and noticed him swallowing something as he spun around to face me. "What's in your hand?" I asked.

He held out a wadded-up Mr. Goodbar wrapper.

"Where's the rest of it?"

"The rest?"

"Jump up and down—like this," I ordered him, bouncing up and down to demonstrate. Pig rolled his eyes but finally joined in. We were both hopping around like a pair of Mexican jumping beans. The soccer team stopped practicing to stare at us. One candy bar, then two, then three fell out of Pig's pockets.

"Just as I thought," I said, picking them up.

"So what? The experiment hasn't officially begun," he protested.

"You're right," I said, handing them back to him. "Go ahead and eat them. We need to get an idea of what

45

you're eating now so we can compare it to what you eat when you start cutting down on fat. Which reminds me, I have some presents for you."

I reached into my backpack and brought out a small book I'd bought for Pig that told you the fat and fiber content of most foods. "Keep this with you at all times. It will help you choose what to eat while you're on the program. I have one just like it at home and I'll be using it to total up the number of fat and fiber grams you eat each day."

Then I reached in again and dug out the little spiral notebook I had brought and held it out to him. "From now on, I want you to write down everything you eat in this notebook, starting with the spaghetti you had for dinner last night."

I started to walk down the street, and he followed, staring at me suspiciously.

"Hey, how did you know what I had for dinner? Are you spying on me or something?"

"No. I don't need to. I just know these things. So you'd better tell me the truth, because I'm going to find out anyway . . . one way or another."

Pig scowled. "I'll tell the truth. But first you have to tell me how you knew what I had for dinner."

"Easy. It's written all over you."

"Huh?"

"Your shirt."

Pig pulled his T-shirt away from his belly and stared at it.

"Hey, you're right." He laughed, pushing his long dark

hair back out of his eyes. "Michael Jordan looks like he has chicken pox. Boy, that was great sauce. My masterpiece," he said, kissing his fingertips. "It was the extra basil that did it. My dad says I'm the Michelangelo of spaghetti sauce."

"C'mon, I'm freezing," I said, tugging on his sleeve. I turned up my collar, shoved my hands into the pockets of my down jacket and started walking toward home.

"Isn't that the same shirt you wore yesterday?" I asked, looking over my shoulder at Pig, who was ambling along a few steps behind me.

"Yeah," Pig said, grinning. "Michael Jordan; he's the Michelangelo of basketball."

"Doesn't your mom make you change clothes?"

"Not unless she catches me before I get out the door. It's a lot easier this way. You take off your clothes at night, drop them on the floor and in the morning they're right there when you need them. No folding, no putting things in drawers or in the laundry hamper. You ought to try it sometime."

"I'll put it on my list of lifetime goals," I said.

We reached the corner. I pushed the button on the stoplight and waited for the Walk signal to start flashing. "It's too bad my mom won't be there when we get to my house. She'd love talking to you," I said.

"Why, does she like to cook too?"

"No. She's a shrink."

"What's your dad do?"

"He's a neurosurgeon. They're both into brains. It's sort of the family business."

47

The traffic stopped and we started across the intersection. The Don't Walk signal started flashing as we reached the middle of the street, and a carload of high-school kids honked at us.

"Hey, blubber boy," the driver called to Pig, leaning out his window. "Speed it up, would you? I'd hate to run into you and hurt my car."

His friends hooted at his joke, and he gunned his engine and squealed past Pig just as he stepped up on the curb. A sharp stab of anger and fear went through me, but Pig didn't react. He went right on talking, as though that kind of thing happened to him every day.

"Does your dad ever bring home any brains?" he asked. "When I was in third grade this kid had a dad who was a scientist who studied brains, and he brought one to class for us to see. It was kind of yellow and wormy looking and it was floating around in a jar."

"My dad lives in Boston," I said. I hoped that might end the conversation, but it didn't.

"I guess he'd have to send it on an airplane then," Pig said. "He'd probably have to buy the brain its own seat so it wouldn't get broken in the baggage compartment. That would really give the flight attendant something to think about. Would your brain like anything to drink?" he said in a squeaky flight-attendant voice.

"Just some formaldehyde, please. Straight up," he answered himself in a deeper voice.

"Would he like a magazine to read?"

"It's not a he, it's a she. And she doesn't have any hands."

"I'm so sorry, sir. I didn't know," said the squeaky voice. "How about some headphones, then?"

His imaginary conversation continued until I turned into our cul-de-sac.

"You live on Riverwood Drive?" Pig asked.

"Six thirty-seven," I said. "The red brick with the circle drive in front."

We walked up the front steps and I unlocked the door, stepped into the foyer and hung my coat in the closet. Pig was still standing in the doorway.

"Wow," he said.

"Come inside. Make yourself at home."

Pig walked past me into the living room. He picked up one of the photographs lined up on the mantel above the fireplace.

"Who's the kid with the swim mask and snorkel?" he asked. "Look at those skinny legs."

"That's me in second grade," I said. "My parents and I were in Hawaii. My dad had to speak at some sort of convention and he took us with him."

"What about this one?" he asked, pointing to a picture of my mom and me sitting in a chairlift with a snow-covered mountain in the background.

"That's the year we were in Switzerland. My dad went there to get an award from the World Science Foundation."

"I thought you said your parents were divorced," he said.

"They are . . . now. Those are just old pictures."

"Do you still get to go on vacations with him?"

I took the picture out of Pig's hands and set it back up on the mantel. "Not since he got married again," I said, straightening the pictures out. "I have a half brother, Henry. He's little and you can't take him anywhere. So I just spend my vacations at their house in Boston. That's where I'm going for Thanksgiving."

"Nice house," Pig said. "I bet you have your own room with your own phone and a television."

I nodded.

"And Nintendo?" he asked.

"No. Only a computer."

"Wow. I mean, nice."

Pig leaned back on the plush sofa cushions and put his arms behind his head. His belly button looked out from under his T-shirt like a third eye.

"Stay right there. Don't move a muscle."

I went over to the corner cabinet, took out my mother's Polaroid camera and aimed it at Pig.

"Say cheese," I said, and snapped the shutter.

Pig looked startled.

"What's that for?"

"It's your 'before' picture," I said. "Now we'll start turning you into an 'after.'"

I left the room and Pig called out after me.

"Why don't we start with an after-school snack instead?"

"Later," I said.

I brought in a stack of magazines and dumped them on the table in front of him.

50

"I've been doing a little research," I said.

"At the library?"

"Yeah. But I got these from the supermarket."

Pig picked up several and read the covers. " 'Miracle Foods That Burn Away Fat,' 'Have the Body You've Dreamed of with Our Twenty-one Day Diet.' Hey, here's one in *The National Tattler* that sounds good: 'The Chocolate Diet: No Willpower Required.' "

"You can take those home to read if you want," I said.

"You mean there's homework?"

"No, but there *will* be a test," I said.

I picked up a copy of *Woman's Journal*, opened it to a page I had marked, picked up a pencil and read the title. " 'When It Comes to Eating Healthfully, How Do You Rate? Take Our Test and Find Out.' I'll read the questions and you give the answers."

Pig leaned back on the sofa, groaning.

"Hey, come on. This is serious. How will I know what to teach you if we don't start by finding out what you already know?"

"Okay, okay," Pig said.

" 'Number one,' " I read. " 'You're at a restaurant having dinner. As a vegetable side dish, would you order: a. creamed spinach, b. buttered broccoli, or c. steamed carrots?' "

"How about: d. catsup?" Pig asked.

"There is no catsup."

"What kind of a restaurant would run out of catsup?"

"I meant catsup isn't a choice for a vegetable."

"Okay. Order me the creamed spinach. But don't expect me to eat it."

I shot him a look and went on to the next question.

" 'Number two. As a snack would you select: a. potato chips, tortilla chips, nuts, buttered popcorn, b. salted pretzels, microwave light popcorn, or c. baked unsalted pretzels, baked potato chips, baked tortilla chips?' "

"Yes."

"You're only supposed to pick one."

"I can't. They're all good. Just write 'all of the above.' "

I slapped the magazine down on the table. "This is *not* a restaurant. I am *not* your waiter. And you are *not* ordering lunch," I said, chopping the air with my hand to emphasize each point. "I'm trying to find out how much you know about things like fat and fiber so you can follow the diet I'm making up for you. Got it?"

Pig folded his arms across his chest. "I was just trying to have some fun," he said, sulking.

"This *is* fun," I said. " 'Number three. For breakfast, would you vote for a. oatmeal with sliced bananas and skim milk, b. bran flakes with sugar and whole milk, or c. poached eggs with Canadian bacon?' "

"Do they allow write-in candidates?"

I closed the magazine and hit my forehead with both hands.

"What's wrong?" Pig asked. "You said I had to tell the truth."

"Forget the test. I already know what I have to teach you about healthy eating: everything," I grumbled as I got up and headed for the stairs.

"All this talk about food is making me hungry," he called out.

"There's one more thing we have to do, and then we'll have a snack."

I had stayed up late the night before making a flip chart to help Pig remember what foods he was supposed to eat, and I was really pretty proud of it. The first page showed the food triangle. Then there was a page that said THE BAD GUYS in big red letters, and underneath that were pictures of all the things you weren't supposed to eat: pop, potato chips, candy bars, ice cream, cookies. They all had stick arms and legs and mean, ugly faces. They were carrying clubs and they were chasing a fat stick figure wearing black shoes and a black baseball cap. After that there was a page that said THE GOOD GUYS and had pictures of all the foods you're supposed to eat. I gave all the milk, fruits and vegetables big bulging muscles. They were led by the tall, orange and handsome Commando Carrot and his green, curly-haired sidekick, Broccoli Boy.

I tucked my flip chart under one arm and the bathroom scale under the other and went back down to the living room, but when I got there, Pig was gone.

"Pig?" I called.

There was no answer. I put down the scale and flip chart and walked back out into the foyer; then I called up the stairs to see if he had followed me to my room.

"Pig, where are you?"

I thought he might have gotten disgusted and gone home, but when I looked in the hallway, his books were still on the bench where he had left them. Then I heard a suspicious noise and followed it into the kitchen. Pig was standing in front of an open cabinet.

"I know you're hungry," I said, trying to be sympathetic, "but you can't have a snack until you learn what to eat."

"I don't need you to teach me about food, Tucker," Pig said. "I've had on-the-job experience."

"This won't take long, I promise."

I closed the cabinet door and steered him out of the kitchen, stopping to put him on the scale so I could write down his weight in my notebook. Then I went to get an easel and pointer from my mother's study and set the flip chart up in front of him in the living room.

First I showed him a picture of the food triangle.

"Here's how you choose what you eat," I said. "You need a lot of bread, pasta, fruits and vegetables, a medium amount of milk, meat and cheese, and a little tiny bit of cookies, candy and fats."

"Okay," he said. "I get it. Are we done now?"

"Not yet."

I flipped over to the next page.

"You see these guys?" I asked, pointing at the evil foods.

"You mean those little candy-bar men?" he asked.

"Right. You know who they are?"

Pig was quiet for a moment, studying them. His face was blank.

"No," he said, slowly shaking his head. "But I think I like them."

I leaned down and whispered in his ear for added drama. "They're the enemy, Pig."

Pig backed away from me.

"They want to terminate you," I said, waving my arms in the air.

"Calm down, Tucker. You're getting a little scary here. Those guys are my friends."

"No they're not," I insisted. "They want to clog up your heart and make it explode. They want to pump you with fat until you're so heavy you can hardly crawl to the refrigerator. They want to turn your belly into a toxic waste dump. What kind of friend would treat you like that?"

I went over to the chart and flipped to the next page.

"Now, these," I said, "these are your friends." I pointed to the picture of Commando Carrot, knocking over a whole troop of enemy M&M's, who were lying on the battlefield with stars in their eyes. Behind them Broccoli Boy was launching cucumber missiles aimed at a cookie encampment.

"From now on, Commando Carrot is your hero. Got it?"

"Uh . . . yeah . . . sure."

"Then repeat after me: 'Commando Carrot is my hero.' "

Pig stared at me with a strange expression on his face.

"Are you feeling all right, Tucker? I think the pressure's getting to you."

" 'Commando Carrot is my hero,' " I said more loudly.

He was alternately eyeing me, then looking out into the hallway, as though he was trying to decide whether or not this was a good time to bolt for the door. Then the phone rang and I went into my mother's study to answer it.

"Tucker, how was school today?"

It was my dad, calling from Boston.

"Same as usual," I said, hoping he wouldn't ask me if that was good or bad. I craned my neck, trying to look around the corner to see if Pig was still in the living room, but the cord wouldn't reach that far.

"I've only got a minute to talk. But I wanted to let you know what time I'll be picking you up for dinner on the twentieth. Did your mom give you my message?"

Pig walked into the room and stood next to me.

"I'm going to get a snack now, okay?" he whispered.

"No!"

"She didn't?" my father said.

"Yes, I mean, I wasn't talking to you."

Pig disappeared around the corner before I could stop him.

"The last seminar is over at around four," my father continued, "but there are some people I need to talk to. I'll drive over and pick you up for dinner around quarter to six. Anything special you'd like to eat?"

"All I can find are celery sticks and stuff," Pig said, stepping back into the room.

"Celery is a healthy snack," I said.

"I'm sure it is, Tucker," my father said, "but I was thinking perhaps we could go out to a restaurant together. How about the Cheesecake Castle?"

"Hurry up, Tucker, I'm starving," Pig said.

"Wait a minute. What?" I said.

"The Cheesecake Castle," my father repeated, beginning to sound a little exasperated.

"Cheesecake is a great choice," I mumbled.

Pig's eyes lit up. "All right! Cheesecake! I'm going to like this diet. Where is it? The refrigerator?"

"No. Wait. It has too much fat in it."

"All right, then," my father said. "Why don't you take some time, think of another restaurant and get back to me? I have patients waiting, so I'd better hang up."

Pig started toward the door again. I reached out to grab him and caught a piece of his sleeve.

"I didn't say you could go yet," I shouted.

"What did you say?" my father sputtered into the phone.

"I said . . . I wish you didn't have to go, Dad. But I know you do."

"I feel the same about you, Tucker. By the way, how's your science fair project going?"

Pig twisted his sleeve loose and made a break for the door.

"It's going to the kitchen," I said. "That is, I'm working on it right now . . . in the kitchen."

"Well, I'll let you get back to work, then. If you need any advice we can talk about it when we have dinner."

I hung up the phone and rushed to the kitchen. When I opened the door, I froze. Pig had a pint of Häagen-Dazs ice cream in each hand. He was holding a spoon sideways in his teeth, like a pirate with a dagger.

"I found the enemy," Pig said, through his teeth. "These guys are never going to bother you again."

57

"Just put the spoon down and no one will get hurt," I said, holding both hands up in front of me and moving slowly toward him.

Pig put the ice cream back in the freezer and dropped the spoon in the sink. "If I wanted a friend who was always taking food away from me, I'd be hanging out with Jonah," he said, scowling.

"I'm only trying to do what's good for you," I said.

"Oh yeah? Well, if it's good for me, why does it feel bad? Maybe we should just forget the whole thing."

"I'm not quitting before I've even begun," I said, putting both hands on my hips. "And even if I wanted to change my topic, Ms. Bodine wouldn't let me. Tomorrow we'll begin the low-fat program. I'll meet you at your locker around noon, and *I'll* bring *both* of our lunches."

CHAPTER 8

"What's in there?" Pig asked, nodding at the brown paper bag in my hand when I appeared at his locker at lunchtime the next day.

"Can't tell you," I said. "It'll spoil the surprise. All I can say is you're going to love it."

"Well, just in case I don't, I'm bringing a backup lunch," Pig said. He reached into his locker and pulled out a familiar greasy brown paper bag. I tried to take it from him, but he held it up high in the air, out of my reach. Suddenly another hand appeared out of nowhere and snatched the bag right out of his outstretched fist.

"Thanks for the lunch, Fatso," Jonah called back over his shoulder.

"Hey, I might need that," Pig yelled after him, but Jonah just laughed and kept on walking.

"Forget it," I said. "At least you won't go hungry."

We went into the lunchroom and looked out over the

talking and laughing heads. It was so full most days that some people had to eat outside on the staircase.

"Great," I sighed. "There are no empty tables to sit at."

"Don't worry," Pig said. "I can take care of that."

He walked over to a table where Mariah Lanford was sitting with her friends.

"Hi, girls," he said. "Mind if I join you?"

I had never actually seen anyone curl their lip quite like Mariah did, and I had to admit I sort of admired her for it.

"Take the whole table," she said, whisking her lunch away. "I was just leaving."

She wheeled around and walked away with all her friends following behind her like sheep.

"*Baa baa,* girls," Pig said. One of them turned around to snort at him.

I sat down across from Pig and laid both of our lunches on the table.

"Don't you ever get tired of people treating you that way?" I asked him.

"You mean the way Mariah treats me? She treats everybody that way. Besides, sometimes it comes in handy. We're the only people in the lunchroom who have a table all to ourselves," he said.

"Well, what did you bring me?" he asked, rubbing his hands together.

"One low-fat cream cheese and sprout sandwich on whole wheat for you," I said, reaching in the bag and setting the sandwich on the table, "and one for me."

Pig just stared at it.

"I can't eat that."

"Why not?"

"It's brown. I don't eat brown food. 'If it's brown—set it down.' That's my rule."

"What about bacon—and chocolate?" I protested.

"Those are exceptions," he said.

"What about liver and onions?"

Pig lifted the top of the sandwich like someone looking for worms under a rock. "Yuuuccchh!"

"What's the matter?"

"You must have dropped it. There's grass stuck to the cream cheese."

"That's not grass. Those are alfalfa sprouts. I never thought you were such a picky eater."

"Alfalfa's what cows eat," he said.

I leaned across the table and folded my hands. "Look. It doesn't matter what color it is, or what other animals eat it. As long as Jonah has your backup lunch, this is the only food you're going to get. So you might as well dig in."

Pig screwed up his face and stared down at the sandwich. "It's got to be better than the salami on dry bread that Jonah gives me. But I'm only taking one little bite."

He closed his eyes and daintily bit off a corner of the sandwich. He chewed slowly; then a strange look crept across his face. His eyes flew wide open. His cheeks puffed up. There was a grumbling noise rising up in his throat and he threw his head back.

I stood up and started backing away from the table. He was going to throw up. I was sure of it.

There was a loud crash as I knocked over my chair,

trying to get away from the table. The kids at the tables near us stopped eating their lunches and turned to stare. When they saw me backing away, they scraped their chairs across the floor trying to get away too.

Suddenly Pig's mouth opened. I closed my eyes and waited for the eruption, but what came out of his mouth wasn't what I expected.

"I love it!" he roared. "This is great."

"You do? It is?"

Pig took another big bite of the sandwich. "Mmmm," he said dreamily, then bit off another hunk. " 'If it's brown—wolf it down.' "

I looked around the room and realized we had become the main attraction in the lunchroom. Everyone was laughing and pointing at us, standing up and craning their necks to see what was going on. Not since Pookie Robbins threw his macaroni and cheese at the ceiling to see if it would stick and it fell into Ms. Bodine's hair had lunch been so much fun for so many people.

Pig ate the rest of the sandwich with enthusiasm, then picked up the bag.

"What else have you got?" he asked, peering inside.

"Just a couple of Nutri-Grain bars. You probably won't like them."

"You never know until you try," he said, opening the wrapper and taking a bite.

"Yummm," he said with sincere appreciation. "These are better than Twinkies. Whoever makes them really knows how to get the filling all the way to the end. Mind if I eat the other one too?"

"Well, it was mine. But if you really want it . . ."

"Thanks," he said, peeling open the crinkly foil wrapper happily.

I took several quick bites out of my sandwich, hoping to get most of it down before he asked for that, too. "Maybe I should do this experiment on myself," I said. "You might not lose any weight, but it looks like I will."

Pig's face relaxed into a smile as he gathered up the wrappers and stuffed them into the empty bag. "You know something, I was wrong. I'm going to like being on this diet. Thanks for the lunch, Tucker."

"No problem," I said, tossing the empty bag into the garbage as we walked out into the hall.

"You could bring the same thing tomorrow, if you want."

"Right, and don't forget to bring a backup lunch."

"Huh? Oh, you mean my protection pizza—for Jonah."

I watched Pig walk down the hall, feeling like something was wrong but not sure what. Pig was eating good food, but his enthusiasm worried me. It wasn't what I'd expected. What if he started eating whole heads of cauliflower or tubs of low-fat cream cheese? Too much of a good thing was a genuine possibility here. After all, I didn't really know much about Pig or what made him overeat. Maybe I had accidentally reset something in his brain. What unknown forces was I meddling with?

CHAPTER 9

Friday afternoon, Ms. Bodine called me down to her office to talk about the proposal I'd dropped off for her that morning. She was sitting at her desk reading it when I walked in, and she motioned for me to sit down while she finished. First her eyes lit up, then her brow furrowed, then her lips pursed. It was as though someone were standing offstage whispering, "Do bewilderment. That's good. Now doubt. Uh-huh. Surprise. Suspicion. Yes!" It was a little like watching television with the sound off and trying to guess what was happening, which might have been entertaining if I hadn't been the subject of this little drama.

"Well," she said finally, leaning back in her chair and folding her hands in her lap. She was wearing a white suit with a leopard-print blouse and there were hand-carved wooden giraffes dangling from her ears.

"You've done a fine job, Tucker, considering how little time you've had to work on this. I can see my confidence in you was well founded. There's a lot of excellent research in here."

She flipped through several pages, then ran her finger down one until she found what she was looking for: " 'One in five American teenagers is overweight.' I had no idea the problem was that widespread."

I nodded, sinking back into the chair. "Widespread. I couldn't have said it better myself."

Ms. Bodine adjusted her glasses. "I've marked a few things that need your attention," she said. "For example, the title: 'America, Land of the Free, Home of the Fat.' Don't you think that's a little . . . flamboyant?"

I shrugged. "Maybe I could tone it down a bit."

"I like your idea of comparing results of a low-fat diet and a low-fat diet that emphasizes high-fiber foods. But what about exercise? Your research shows it plays an important role in weight control."

"Well . . . ," I said slowly, "I could do a third comparison with low-fat diet plus exercise." As far as I knew, Pig didn't play any sports, but maybe I could talk him into jogging. I'd seen him run pretty fast when he was trying to get away from Jonah.

"Why don't you give that some thought?" Ms. Bodine said. "By the way, I'm glad your report mentioned the social pressures that encourage some children to go too far with weight loss. Your suggestion about concentrating on health and fitness, not appearance, seems like a good idea."

I started to boost myself out of the chair to make a quick exit, but then she turned the page to the last section. "There's just one more thing I wanted to check. You've got the materials and procedures outlined fairly well. But what do you mean by the 'experimental subject'? You haven't specified that."

"What do you mean what do I mean?"

She folded her arms on the desk.

"I assume you'll want to carefully monitor your subject's food intake. Are you going to use something like a rat?"

"More like a pig," I mumbled. "I mean a Pighetti . . . Angelo Pighetti."

Ms. Bodine took off her glasses and shielded her eyes with one hand, as though she were looking into a bright light.

"You're going to use a *human* subject?" she said. "A student?"

"Umm, actually, yes."

She sighed and leaned back in her chair. "I assume Angelo is a willing subject, at least?"

"Oh, he's very enthusiastic. As a matter of fact, he's getting more excited all the time."

Ms. Bodine smoothed her ink-black hair and flipped back through my proposal; then she closed it and laid it on the desk. "Tucker, frankly, this whole thing worries me a little, especially after what we've just gone through with the handwriting analysis project. There's always an ethical question to consider when you're using human subjects."

"Don't worry, Ms. Bodine. I understand. Science is a tool for helping people."

She rubbed her fingers on the upholstered arms of her chair. "Your father's a doctor, isn't he?" she asked. "A neurologist?"

I nodded.

"Then perhaps you know that one of the most important things people in the healing professions learn is this." She opened her drawer, took out a sheet of paper with her letterhead on it and wrote something in big letters. Then she spun the paper around on her desk so it faced me. "Read it to me, Tucker."

"It says: 'First, do no harm.' "

"Mmmhmmm," Ms. Bodine said, nodding significantly. "I'm going out on a limb for you, Tucker. Way out. Remember that."

She put the sheet of paper on top of my proposal and handed it to me. "I want you to turn in a progress report every week . . . and keep me posted on everything you do."

"I won't forget," I said, tucking the proposal under my arm as I stood up to leave. I couldn't even if I tried.

CHAPTER 10

By the time Pig had been on the low-fat portion of the diet for one week, I had pretty much decided that the problem wasn't going to be teaching him what to eat. It was going to be getting him to eat it. His food diary looked like an excerpt from *Gourmet* magazine, and when I counted up his fat grams, they were off the charts. So I wasn't really surprised when I discovered at the end of the week that he hadn't lost an ounce.

I had to find a way to get him to stick to low-fat foods. Something told me that I needed to observe Pig in his natural habitat—maybe even meet his family. My mother always said the apple doesn't fall far from the tree. Perhaps it was time to stop studying the fruit and go take a look at the orchard. We were about to leave for Pig's house after school to do just that when I heard a familiar voice behind us.

"What do you call it when a giant biscuit falls out of the

sky and smashes Pig and Tucker?" Jonah asked the kid walking with him as he shadowed us.

"I dunno," his friend Brian Woomer said.

"Hitting two nerds with one scone."

Jonah laughed heartily at his own joke.

"What's a scone?" Woomer asked.

"It's a biscuit, stupid."

"Maybe you'd better tell him what a nerd is too," I said, glancing over my shoulder. "I don't think he gets it."

Woomer stared at me with his mouth hanging open. He looked like a bulldog with a lobotomy.

"Okay," Jonah sneered. "A nerd is someone that hangs out with Angelo Pighetti. I knew you didn't have many friends, Shrink, but I didn't think you'd stoop this low."

"Would you mind not calling me Shrink?" I asked.

"Oh yeah, I forgot. Your mom's the one who's the shrink. I guess that makes you the shrinkee. Now, why don't you run along so I can have a talk with Pig?"

I stood my ground, even when he stepped so close to me that he could have rested his chin on top of my head.

"It's all right, Tucker. Jonah doesn't want to start anything," Pig said.

"Get out of my way," Jonah snarled at me.

"Then again," Pig said, "maybe he does."

Jonah was staring at me with his cold blue eyes. I wanted to look away but my eyes locked on his.

"Just tell me one thing," I said, beginning to get nervous. "Did you kill your dog?"

Jonah reached out, grabbed my collar with his fist and

twisted it hard. Then an arm wrapped around his shoulder.

"Jonah," Mr. Albert said, "I think we'd better have a little talk—in my office. Mr. Woomer, would you like to join us?"

It was the first time since I'd turned in my handwriting analysis proposal that I'd been happy to see Mr. Albert. Pig and I had started to walk toward the door when Beth Ellen Hertzel caught up with us. She was wearing black fishnet stockings and a short purple sweater that matched her hair. She glanced nervously down the hall at Jonah, then back at me.

"Be careful, Tucker. He's *dangerous,*" she whispered darkly. "I told Mr. Albert he was bothering you. Didn't Angelo warn you about him?"

"Yeah. He told me some story he said you got from an aunt of yours who works at Gordon."

"Actually," Beth Ellen admitted, "she doesn't work there. But she lives in the town Gordon is in . . . or at least she used to . . . when she was ten."

"Well, that's enough for me," I said.

Beth Ellen pushed her hair back behind her ears, revealing an assortment of silver earrings. "But I personally have traveled there on the astral plane."

"Is that sort of like a Boeing seven forty-seven?" I asked.

"It's another dimension," she sniffed. "I learned how to enter it from Swami Viveswan. That's Ben Goldberg's astral name."

"You're way over my head, Beth Ellen."

"Look, Tucker, I know you think I'm weird."

Wow, I thought, maybe she *is* psychic.

"All I can tell you is, I'm picking up some very strong negative vibrations from him." She closed her eyes and shivered a little. I noticed that her purple eye shadow matched her hair and sweater perfectly. "Don't say I didn't warn you," she said. She hugged her books to her chest as she spun around to leave.

"Beth Ellen is totally amazing," I said, shaking my head.

Pig stared at her with big moony eyes. "Amazing," he repeated. "Don't you love to say her name? It sounds like a waterfall. Bethellenbethellenbethellen."

"We'd better get going," I said, but he didn't move. "Pig?"

"Huh? Oh, right. We can go out the back door." He came to and started walking in the other direction.

"Hey, wait," I called out. "That's the wrong way. You told me you lived on the other side of Washington Street."

"I know, but we're going to have to take a detour so we won't run into Jonah. Mr. Albert's not going to do us much good once we leave the school grounds."

We went out through the loading dock, then down the alley to Carpenter Street, past the Dairy Queen, Bett's Bakery, Katie's Country Candy Store and Dunkin' Donuts. All Pig's landmarks seemed to have a lot of calories in them, and each time we passed one, the people inside smiled and waved at him. I was beginning to wonder if Pig had some other reason for taking this route home. Especially when we got to Frankie's Pizzeria and Grocery and Pig turned to go in.

"Hold it," I said. "We're not stopping until we get to your house."

"This *is* my house," he said.

"You live in a grocery store?"

"No. I live above a grocery store. My parents sell pizza and stuff. We live upstairs. That's how I know so much about cooking. Your family's into brains, my family's into bellies."

On the door there was a sign that said, NO SHOES. NO SHIRT. NO SWEAT, which right away tells you a lot about Frankie's Pizza. On one side of the store there was an Italian grocery: three aisles of shelves filled with imported oil, crusty bread, plum tomatoes, pasta, espresso and tins of olives as big as gallons of milk.

Along the wall, there was a deli case filled with cheeses so strong you could smell them when you walked in the door and lunch meat that Pig said people in Italy use to scare off vampires. The deli case was decorated with plastic grapevines, little twinkly white lights, and big brown sausages that hung on strings from the ceiling. Next to the deli there was a big freezer filled with tubs of gelato: lemon, lime, strawberry, chocolate, kiwi, pistachio. You name it, they froze it. The walls in back were covered with posters from Italian operas, and there were tables filled with people wagging their fingers in each other's faces. They were talking loudly in several languages, trying to be heard above a recording of a soprano that was playing in the background.

It was as busy as the freeway at rush hour. A line of customers was standing at the counter, shouting orders for pepperoni pizza or espresso or Italian ice, while the people behind the counter rushed back and forth to and from the kitchen to fill them. As we walked in the front door, Mrs. Pighetti came out of the kitchen, wearing a white dress, with rolls and rolls of white flesh flowing out of the armholes and the neck. She looked like a mountain of Marshmallow Fluff.

"Angelo, *bambino,*" she said, wrapping her arms around him in an enormous hug. "Who's your friend?"

Before I could answer, the marshmallow arms closed in on me and everything went black. There was soft, white flesh covering my eyes, squashing my nose, and pressing against my teeth.

"Whatsa matter? Is he shy?"

"Let him go, Mama," Pig said. "How can he talk to you? He can't even breathe."

The marshmallow arms released their grip. I knew now that I was in over my head. I was up against something big, something powerful, something no one could resist.

"This is Tucker Harrison, Mama," Pig said as I stood there gasping for breath.

"Nice to meet you, Tucker," she said. Then she took both of my cheeks in her hands and pinched them.

"Ow!" I protested.

"Don't worry," Pig said. "You'll get used to it."

"Let's go have a snack," she said, putting her arms around me and steering me toward the kitchen.

"Hey, Papa," Mrs. Pighetti called to a man taking pizza out of the oven with a big wooden paddle. "Angelo brought a friend home. This is Tucker."

73

"Nice to meet you, Pucker," Mr. Pighetti said, wiping his hands on his apron before holding one out to me.

"No, Papa, Tucker," Pig corrected him.

"Pucker, Tucker. What's the difference?" he said. Then he leaned over the counter, held Pig's head in an armlock and rubbed his head with his knuckles. Mr. Pighetti looked a lot like Angelo, only bigger. With their arms around each other that way, they looked like a couple of sumo wrestlers with clothes on.

"It's been so busy today I can't even think straight. Angelo, there's some leftover spaghetti. Why don't you boys have some? Tooker's hungry, aren't you, Tooker?"

"It's Pucker," I said. "I mean, Tucker." Then because it looked like he was going to give me an armlock, too, I added, "Just call me anything you like."

"Okay, Mr. Tucker Pucker Harrison. Our house is your house. Pull up a stool."

Pig and I sat down to eat our pasta, while Mr. Pighetti used one hand to take big circles of dough, pour tomato sauce on them and sprinkle them with cheese, then with the other hand opened the oven door to check on the pizza he was baking. I had never seen anyone do so much, so fast, with only two hands.

"So, Pucker, you live in the neighborhood?" Mr. Pighetti asked, popping a piece of pepperoni in his mouth before attacking an onion with a large, wooden-handled knife.

"On Riverwood Drive," I said.

"Nice place," Mr. Pighetti said. "We've got some delivery customers over there. We ever deliver to you?"

"Probably not," I said. "When we eat out, it's mostly Chinese."

"That's because you've never tasted Frankie's pizza with Angelo's homemade sauce. My son," he said, holding Pig's face in both hands and planting a big wet kiss on his lips. "The best Italian cook in the city."

"Cut it out, Papa," Pig said, trying to pull his head away.

"Hey, what's so bad about being proud of your son? Tell you what, Tucker. Next time your family feels like pizza, call us and dinner's on the house. Compliments of Angelo. We'll just take it out of his paycheck."

"Yeah. Like you ever give me a paycheck, Papa."

"When your family owns a pizza parlor . . . ," Mr. Pighetti began.

"I know, I know," Pig said. "Everybody's gotta pitch in."

"Besides," Mr. Pighetti said, "most kids would love having a job like yours. They'd probably do it for nothing, just because it's so much fun. Right, Tucker?"

Pig and his father both stared at me, waiting for me to cast the deciding vote. I gulped down the last bite of my pasta, trying to think of a response that would satisfy them both.

"I guess so. I mean, I've never done anything like this, so I don't really know how much fun it would be."

Mr. Pighetti blinked with disbelief.

"You never made a pizza?"

"No."

"You ever wait tables?"

75

"No."

"You ever take down an order? Make espresso? Dish up gelato?"

I shook my head.

"Perfect. You're hired. Come on," he said, guiding me out through the kitchen door into the restaurant. "Let me show you around the amusement park."

There was a short dark man slicing cheese behind the deli counter, and Mr. Pighetti called out to him.

"José, we need to borrow your apron for the new employee," he said, slapping me on the back. "He's just about your size."

"*Sí*, Senor Pighetti," Jose said. He took his apron off, then came over and slipped it over my head, with a lot of ceremony, as though it were a great honor. "Looking good. Very nice," he said, spinning me around to check the side angles.

Then Mr. Pighetti pointed me toward the far corner of the restaurant. "Now for the fun part. You see those three tables over there by the window?" he said. "They got your name on them. Go get 'em."

He wheeled around to go back to the kitchen, and I went after him.

"Wait," I said. "I don't know what to do."

Mr. Pighetti smiled and threw both hands in the air.

"Of course not," he said. "If you knew what you were doing, you wouldn't be here."

He put his arm around my shoulder and walked me out toward the tables.

"I'll let you in on a little secret," he said. "When you're a kid, you think you're the only one who doesn't know anything; that just because the grown-ups are bigger, that means they've figured everything out. But the truth is, nobody knows what they're doing. Everybody else is muddling around too, trying to figure it all out, trying to do a better job. And they're all afraid they're going to do something stupid, or make a mess of things, just like you."

"But . . ."

"Don't worry," Mr. Pighetti said, patting me on the back. "The best thing about falling down is it gives you a chance to practice getting up."

He handed me a pad of paper and a pencil.

"Now go take Mr. Kleinkopf's order. That guy there. He's a regular, so treat him nice."

Mr. Kleinkopf was sitting in the corner facing the door, wearing a rumpled charcoal suit with an old gray sweater underneath and a tie covered with purple flowers and green and red tropical birds. He wore an old black cap with a visor, but you could see his gray hair curling out beneath it. I took a deep breath and walked slowly to his table.

"Mr. Kleinkopf?" I asked.

He looked up at me, then pulled his suit coat over his head.

"Who are you?" he growled at me from beneath the coat. "How do you know my name?"

"I'm the new waiter," I said.

Mr. Kleinkopf rubbed his gray stubbled face with his hand and stared at me, his watery brown eyes turning darker.

"You expect me to believe that?" he said. "Where's José, what have you done with him?"

"He's right over there," I said, pointing toward the deli counter. But when I looked, there was no one there.

"Well, he *was* there," I said.

Mr. Kleinkopf lowered the suit coat a little and sneered.

"I'm a friend of Pig's," I said, hoping to convince him he could trust me.

"You talk to pigs?" he asked, pulling the coat back up.

"I mean Angelo," I corrected myself. "Angelo Pighetti. His friends call him Pig."

Mr. Kleinkopf relaxed and lowered his coat.

"Hmph! Some friends," he said. "Why didn't you tell me who you were in the first place? I'm an old man. You could have given me a heart attack."

He motioned for me to come closer, then whispered in my ear.

"I'll have the usual . . . and don't try anything funny."

"The usual," I repeated, "nothing funny."

I walked back to the kitchen and stuck my head in the door.

"Mr. Kleinkopf wants the usual, whatever that is."

"Hey, nice going, Mr. I-don't-know-what-to-do. Angelo, dish up some of that calamari for Mr. Kleinkopf, will you?"

Pig picked up a plate and filled it with noodles, then

ladled some red soupy stuff from a big black pot on top of them. He handed me the plate. I took one look at it and had to turn the other way.

"There's something disgusting in there," I said, handing the plate back to him. "I think something fell in the pot."

Pig stared at the plate in his hand.

"What? I don't see anything."

"Those things with the suckers on them," I said, trying not to look directly at them. "It doesn't look like they're moving, so I guess they're already dead. But you'd better call the exterminator. They probably travel in packs."

Pig rolled his eyes up to the ceiling and waved his free hand in the air. "That's the calamari, Tucker. Those are their tentacles."

"Yuck. Do you eat the females, too?" I asked.

"I said, *ten*tacles, Tucker," he said, sighing. "Calamari is squid."

"Mr. Kleinkopf eats tentacles from a squid?"

Pig nodded. "Every time he comes in here, which is almost every day."

I stared down at the sucker-covered arms reaching up out of the depths of the tomato sauce.

"So that's what's wrong with him," I mumbled.

I walked back out of the kitchen and set the plate down on the table.

"One usual, nothing funny," I said.

Mr. Kleinkopf grabbed me by the arm. "Wait." He scowled at me. "How do I know it's safe to eat this?"

I thought Mr. Kleinkopf was crazy, but he was beginning to make sense. I reached for the plate but he stopped me.

"Ha! I thought so. You've slipped something in here, haven't you?"

"No, honest. I know it looks like something slipped in there, but Pig said it's supposed to look like that."

"Sit down," he commanded, pulling out a chair for me. He stabbed one of the sucker-covered things with his fork and held it up in the air. "You first," he said.

"N-N-No thanks," I stammered, pushing my chair back. "I . . . uh . . . don't really like tentacles."

He moved the fork closer to my mouth, as though he were waiting for me to open it. I was afraid to protest again for fear he might pop it in. The wiggly white tentacle came closer and closer. I couldn't take my eyes off it. My head was swimming and I felt like I was going to pass out. Luckily, a hand swooped out of the air and plucked it off the fork.

"Mmmmm," Pig said, popping it into his mouth and swallowing. "Nice and rubbery, just the way you like it, Mr. Kleinkopf." Then he turned to me.

"Didn't you hear Papa calling you, Tucker? He wants you in the kitchen right away."

Pig studied my face as we turned to leave the table. "You look a little green," he said.

"I'll be okay. Just keep that tentacle-eater away from me."

"Tucker, what took you so long?" Mr. Pighetti said as I walked back into the kitchen. "I want you to put that bread in a bag and take it out to Louie." He tipped his head in the direction of a pile of stale crusts on the counter.

"How do I know which one Louie is?"

"Easy," said Pig, who was ladling up a bowl of calamari for himself. "He's the one with the pigeon on his head."

"I didn't see anyone in there with a pigeon on his head," I said.

"That's because he's outside. Do you think I'd let a pigeon in my restaurant?" Mr. Pighetti said, whirling his arms in the air like eggbeaters. "Angelo, maybe you'd better go with him."

"Okay, okay," Pig said, setting down his bowl. We took the bread crumbs and went out the back door of the kitchen. There was a small garden behind the building with a border of red and gold flowers and a few tables in the center shaded by a tree. Beneath the tree there was a man sitting perfectly still with his hands held palms up on either side of him. His face was tan and wrinkled, even though he seemed to be about my father's age. His hair was long, blond, slicked back and thinning at the top, and he had eyes the color of the sky that stared straight ahead. A large flock of birds was flying around him and pecking at the ground beneath his feet. Some of them were sitting on his head and shoulders, and others flew down and pecked food from his open hands, then skittered away. He was kind of like a human bird feeder.

Pig waited while I walked closer to the man. There was a great squawking and flutter of wings as the birds took off and rearranged themselves in new patterns. I stood in the center of the flock, not knowing what to do next.

"Go ahead, put the bread in his hands," Pig said.

"Louie?" I whispered.

The human bird feeder sat perfectly still, as though we weren't even there.

"Mr. Pighetti asked me to bring these to you," I said a little more loudly. I felt foolish, but I took the bag and poured the bread crumbs into his hands anyway, watching his face carefully for any movement or sign of recognition. But he just stared blankly ahead, looking right through me.

As I backed away, the circling flock of birds settled back on Louie's arms and head with a great flapping of wings, all fighting for a space near the bread crumbs.

"Louie says thanks. The birds do too," Pig said.

"Everyone here is crazy," I said, not realizing Mr. Pighetti had come from the kitchen and was standing behind me, watching.

"Secret number two," he said, putting an arm around my shoulder and holding two fingers up in front of my face. "Everyone everywhere is crazy. It's just that most of them don't know it yet."

CHAPTER 11

When I came home from school the next day, there was a silver Lexus parked in our driveway. I knew as soon as I walked in the front door that it must belong to my dad. My mother was in the living room talking, and there was something about her voice that pulled me back to the days when they were still married. I felt like I was lying in my bed again as their voices drifted up the stairs through the darkness: her shouting, his footsteps walking out of the room, and the long silence after.

"I can't believe you would do this, Alex," she said.

I closed the door and put my books down on the hall table, but my parents were too wrapped up in their conversation to notice.

"You can't just take him down and admire him and then put him back on the shelf like some sort of trophy."

When my dad answered, his voice was lower, muffled. He spoke so softly, I couldn't make out what he said, only my mother's angry response.

"Then you'll have to talk to him about this yourself," she said.

"Talk to me about what?" I asked, walking into the living room.

My mother's face was a confusion of emotions. "Tucker! I didn't expect you this early. I thought you were going to Ms. Bodine's office after school to drop off a copy of your preliminary research for your science fair project."

"I did, but she was out of the building, so I to decided to go back Monday."

"Hello, son," my father said, standing up to greet me. He was wearing a black pinstripe suit that made his thick gray hair look almost white.

I hung back, not knowing whether to shake his hand or let him hug me, either of which would have felt strange just then, and finally decided to avoid the problem by slumping down in a chair.

"Hi, Dad. I thought you weren't coming until next week."

He sat down again and took off his glasses to clean them with his handkerchief.

"I changed my schedule to be on a panel tomorrow afternoon," he said. "I have to fill in for someone who was called out of the country. But I have some free time tonight. I thought perhaps we could go out to a restaurant together."

"Sure," I said, shrugging.

"Why don't you go upstairs and get cleaned up?" my

mom said. "Would you like some coffee while you wait, Alex? I have some made in the kitchen."

"Thank you, no. But if I could use your phone . . . ?"

"Of course," she said. "Use the one in my office if you like."

My mom came over and kissed me on the top of my head.

"Be sure and bring him home at a decent time," she said to my father. "You have homework, don't you, Tucker?"

"A little," I said.

I started to go upstairs and then remembered what I had overheard when I came in.

"What was it you wanted to tell me?" I asked, not even sure I wanted to know the answer. My mom gave my father an icy look as she left to go into the kitchen.

"We've got a lot to talk about," Dad said. "Why don't you get ready and we'll discuss everything over dinner."

Somehow I felt that I wasn't going to have much of an appetite. It looked like our dinner wasn't the only thing that was going to get grilled. When I came back downstairs, my father was out in the car waiting.

"Where would you like to go?" he asked as I settled into the beige leather seat and slammed the door.

"I really like the Hunan Palace," I said, thinking that at least then I'd be in friendly territory. "It's on Tenth Street."

"Yes, I know," my father said. "It used to be your mother's favorite."

"It still is," I said, searching his face for some kind of clue to what he was feeling. "Does that mean you don't want to go there?"

A thin smile spread across his face as he turned the key in the ignition.

"Not at all," he said, turning out of the driveway into the street. "Despite what your mother may have told you, I don't make all my decisions by doing the opposite of whatever she would like."

"I didn't mean that," I said, turning to watch some kids playing in a pile of leaves at the corner of our street.

"I know," he said. "I'm sorry. That was misdirected. Three years of living in separate cities hasn't made it any easier for your mother and me to get along. But I don't want that to spoil what little time we have together, Tucker. Let's put it behind us, shall we? Tell me what you've been doing lately."

"Not much. School, homework . . . oh, and I learned how to be a waiter yesterday."

"You have a job?" my father said, surprised.

"I was just helping out a friend. His family owns a restaurant and Italian grocery, and he invited me there after school."

"Tucker, if you need more money, I'd be glad to provide it. I really think your time would be better spent studying than working in your friend's deli."

"I didn't do it for money, Dad. Although I might want to get a job sometime."

"School is your job, Tucker. You don't need another one to distract you from learning what you really need to know—unless you want to spend the rest of your life making pizzas."

"Some people do."

"Not people like us," he said as he slowed down for a stoplight. We both sat staring at the car ahead of us while we waited for the light to turn green. "What are you thinking about?" he asked finally.

A picture popped into my mind of my father reading a social studies book with one of those picture maps of all the people on earth. Only on his map, there was one tiny little space with green stick figures labeled "people like us," and the rest of the world was filled with red stick figures labeled "everybody else."

"Nothing," I mumbled.

"Dr. Harrison. What a happy surprise," Mr. Wong said, stretching his hand out to shake my father's as we walked into the Hunan Palace.

"It's good to see you, Mr. Wong. I don't get into town as often as I'd like to, now that I'm in Boston."

"Ahhh, yes. Your new job. So many changes in your life." Mr. Wong looked down at me, then back at my father. "It is best for all of us to learn to adapt," he said.

I saw some expression flicker over my father's face, but it passed so quickly I couldn't tell what it was.

"Do you have a table for us?" my father asked. "I'm sorry we didn't make a reservation, but this was all rather last-minute."

Mr. Wong put his arm around me as he steered me toward our usual table.

"There is always room in the Hunan Palace for Dr. Harrison and his guests," he said, smiling.

We slid into the booth and Mr. Wong handed us our menus.

"I recommend the lichee duck tonight," he said. "Very fresh and crisp, with just a hint of spice."

My father glanced at the menu and then closed it.

"I'd prefer shrimp," he said. "Would you serve the vegetables separately? And perhaps some hot and sour soup to start with."

"Certainly, Dr. Harrison. And for you, Tucker? The usual?"

"I think I'll have the duck," I said. "It sounds good."

Mr. Wong raised his eyebrows and glanced at me out of the corner of his eye.

"Very well," he said, taking our menus back. "Shrimps for Dr. Harrison and lichee duck for his adventuresome son."

"Well, let's hear about your science fair project," my father said when Mr. Wong had left. "I spoke to Ms. Bodine earlier in the week and she told me you'd selected a new topic. She seems to think it's a good one, too, although she didn't share any of the details with me."

I could feel my face grow hot and was glad it was dark so my father wouldn't notice my cheeks turning red. "You called her without even telling me?" I asked.

"Actually she called me. I told her I wanted to be kept abreast of your progress. After that handwriting analysis fiasco, I felt it was important for someone to monitor your schoolwork . . . someone in the family."

"You had no right to do that," I said, glaring at him.

His eyes fixed firmly on mine.

"I had every right. I'm still your father, even if I live in another state." I must have looked as though he'd slapped me because his face suddenly softened. "It's just that I'm concerned about you, Tucker. We may be separated, but you're still my son and I want to do whatever I can to help you be successful."

Mr. Wong appeared with our soup, and my father leaned back in his seat and folded his hands.

"Would you mind bringing us a pot of tea?" my father asked, without looking up. He waited until Mr. Wong had left before he spoke again. "I hope you're taking it seriously this time, Tucker. Your project . . . what is it? Something about nutrition?"

"Nutrition and obesity," I said.

"Ms. Bodine seems to like it. But are you sure you have a good grasp on the subject? I don't need to tell you how important it is that you make a good showing at the science fair."

"No," I said, making whirlpools in the soup with my spoon. "I think you've made that part pretty clear."

"If you need any help I can get someone down at the hospital to talk to you. One of the dietitians, perhaps. Or I could have the medical library do a computer search."

We were interrupted a moment by Mr. Wong, who set our dinner plates down in front of us.

"I'm already doing my own research, Dad," I said. Then

I hesitated. "Mom's given me some good ideas too," I added.

My father pushed a bite of shrimp onto his fork with his knife, then chewed it while he thought about this.

"Yes . . . well," he said finally. "Your mother and I have different philosophies. Sometimes you need additional perspectives."

There was a long silence while we both picked at our meals. Neither one of us, it seemed, wanted to talk about the differences between my mother and my father. My dad put down his fork and wiped his mouth with the linen napkin, then poured himself a cup of tea.

"How soon will you have something written up?" he asked.

"I have a progress report due on Monday, but I won't have the research written up for several weeks."

"Send it to me at my office when it's done, will you? I'm looking forward to reading it," he said in his chairman's voice, bringing the meeting to a close. "Oh, and there's one more thing I wanted to talk to you about."

My father set the white china cup down and stared at the tea leaves that remained at the bottom as though he were looking for an answer in them. He brushed some crumbs off the tablecloth and sat silently awhile before he looked at me again.

"I'm afraid there's been a change in plans for Thanksgiving, Tucker. That's what your mother and I were discussing earlier. I've been asked to speak at a conference at Oxford that week. It's the only chance I'll have to meet with the coauthor of the book I'm working on before he leaves for Hong Kong."

A flood of feelings washed over me, all mixed together in a murky wave so I couldn't tell one from another.

"Why would anyone want to have a conference at Thanksgiving?" I said, as much to myself as to my father.

He smiled at me the way you'd smile at a little kid. "Thanksgiving isn't a holiday in England as it is here," he said. "You can still come to Boston, of course. Madelyn's parents are coming in from Concord. She's looking forward to having you there too. So is Henry."

"No thanks," I said. "I'll come and visit you another time—when you're actually there."

He felt the sting of my words and sat up stiffly, then tried to smooth things over.

"I know how disappointed you must be," he said. "I am too, Tucker. Our time together is important to me. It's just that my plans don't always work out."

I pushed the food around on my plate and said nothing.

"I might be able to see you once more before the science fair, though. Maybe I can arrange a layover."

Mr. Wong reappeared and set down a plate with two fortune cookies. "The duck was not to your liking?" he asked, glancing down at my plate, which was still half full.

"Actually it was good. I was just too busy talking to eat it all. Maybe I could bring it home."

"Certainly," said Mr. Wong. "And take this, too," he added, handing me a small red book. "I have been saving this for you, Tucker. It will answer some of the questions you had the other night."

I turned the book over and read the cover. "*The Handbook of Chinese Horoscopes*. Hey, thanks. This looks really interesting."

My father folded his arms on the table and drummed his fingers as I flipped through the pages. "Would you please bring us a check, Mr. Wong? I'm afraid I'm in a bit of a hurry tonight."

"Of course, Dr. Harrison," Mr. Wong said, tipping his head in my father's direction.

My father pushed the plate of fortune cookies to my side of the table. I cracked a cookie open and unfolded the little slip of paper inside, then read it out loud. " 'If a fool persists in his folly, he may become wise.' Hmm . . . looks like I'm on the right track. Here," I said, pushing the plate back toward my father. "Don't you want yours?"

"No. I've sworn off desserts," he said, patting his stomach.

"You can at least read it. No one ever got fat reading his fortune."

He broke open the remaining cookie, glanced at the paper and smiled.

"What does it say?" I asked.

" 'Wise men are not always learned. Learned men are not always wise.' I wonder," my father said, "if Mr. Wong writes these fortunes himself."

CHAPTER 12

The way things were going, I wasn't looking forward to going into Ms. Bodine's office on Monday to turn in my progress report. So I was relieved when Ms. Bodine's secretary asked me to leave it in her mailbox.

"She said to tell you she'll look it over and get back to you. Right now she's meeting with the other contestant for the science fair."

"I didn't know there was another contestant from our school," I said, surprised." Who is he?"

"It's not a he," the secretary said. "It's—"

"Beth Ellen!" I said as the door to the outer office opened and she appeared. "Why were you in there with the science fair contestant?"

"I *am* the science fair contestant," she said dryly.

"You? I didn't know you liked science."

"Only some kinds of science," she said. "I like to commune with other living things—to help them grow. It's our only hope for saving the global life system we all share."

"We'll all sleep easier tonight knowing you're on the case," I said as we walked out of the office together.

"I'll overlook your sarcasm, knowing that it's only an indication of your need for enlightenment, Tucker. Would you like to see my project?"

"Sure, why not? It never hurts to know what the competition is like."

Pig caught up with us as we made our way down the hall to the science lab.

"Hi, Beth Ellen," he said. "I like your hair with all those stripes of color. You remind me of a rainbow."

She smiled at him, and he leaned closer and sniffed her hair.

"Mmmm," he said, breathing deeply, "it smells good too . . . like Hawaiian Punch."

Beth Ellen laughed. "It must be the mango shampoo I use."

He licked his lips. "Juicy, sweet mangoes. Can't you just taste them?"

"You're so sensual, Angelo," Beth Ellen said. "I love that about you. I was just going to show Tucker my science fair project. It's right in here," she said, opening the door to the science lab and leading us over to a table by the window where there was a large container filled with mud.

"Gee, Beth Ellen. That's a really nice box of dirt," I said.

"It's not *just* dirt, Tucker. It's a worm garden."

"Always doing the unexpected, aren't you, Beth Ellen?

Everyone else has flowers in their garden. But not you. You're growing worms."

"You have no idea how important worms are," Beth Ellen said. "If it weren't for worms, plants would have nothing to eat. They're like little compost factories. I feed them garbage, and they gobble it all up and turn it into this stuff." She reached in the box and scooped up a handful of dirt. "Worm castings."

"You mean worm doodoo?"

"To you, it's doodoo." Beth Ellen sniffed. "But to a plant, it's a gourmet meal."

"Wow," Pig said, "they're in the restaurant business like me." He was leaning over with his face close to the dirt to get a better look at them.

"That's a great way of looking at it," Beth Ellen said, taking out a piece of paper and pencil to jot it down. "I think I'll use that in my report. I'm going to write about how worm gardens and other organic methods can increase food production. What are you doing your science fair project on, Tucker?"

"Mine's about food too. It's on nutrition and obesity."

"Do you think worms have to worry about getting fat like I do?" Pig asked, picking one up from a hole he'd scratched in the dirt and holding it in the palm of his hand.

"Worms don't worry about anything, and you shouldn't either, Angelo," Beth Ellen said. "I think you're wonderful the way you are."

Pig seemed to be falling under some kind of spell. He had this dazed look in his eyes.

"I was just thinking," Pig said. "Maybe you could come to the restaurant sometime and give us advice about our garden. It's gotten kind of run-down since my grandfather died."

"Was your grandfather a good gardener?"

"My father says he could spit a peach pit on the ground, and the next day there'd be a tree there. When he was young, he was a caretaker at Isola Bella. That means 'beautiful island' in Italian. It was just a pile of rocks until Count Carlo fell in love with Isabella in the 1500s and built her a palace there. Now it has a terraced garden with statues and fountains, and there are peacocks running all around it."

"It sounds beautiful, Angelo."

"Ever since my grandfather died, I keep having this dream that I'm out working in the garden behind the restaurant, watering and pulling weeds, but the plants aren't growing very well. Then my grandpa walks up. 'Where've you been, Grandpa?' I ask him. And he says, 'I've been in heaven. Where do you think I've been?' I ask him what he does all day in heaven, and he says he works in the garden, because what you do in heaven is pretty much what you learned to be good at on earth. Then I ask him why he came back. And my grandpa says, 'There's one thing I forgot to tell you, Angelo. It's important you know this if you want to be a good gardener.' "

There was a long silence. "Well," I said, running out of patience, "what is it?"

Pretending I wasn't there, Pig looked directly into Beth Ellen's eyes.

" 'Remember the worms, Angelo.' That's what he said to me."

Beth Ellen blinked and stared back at him. I couldn't tell whether she thought Pig's dream was wonderful, or the stupidest thing she'd ever heard.

"Well, I'd better get going," she said.

"Wait," Pig said, reaching out for her arm. "Do you mind if I smell your hair one more time? I'm really hungry."

"Of course not. And you can have this, too," she said, rummaging in her purse and bringing out half of a sandwich. "I wasn't hungry enough to eat the whole thing at lunch."

Pig's eyes lit up as he took the sandwich from her. "Hey, cream cheese and sprouts! My favorite."

Angelo watched Beth Ellen walk away, a vision in purple and black.

"She's really one of a kind," I said.

"Yeah," he said dreamily. "That's what I like about her."

I could see he was going to be lost in his fantasies for a while, so I pulled out *The Handbook of Chinese Horoscopes* and started to read it as we walked together down the hall.

"What are you reading about?" Pig said when he finally roused himself.

"I'm trying to find out what kind of person I am," I murmured, holding my place with one finger.

"You have to look in a book for that? If *you* don't know what kind of person you are, how can you expect the book to know?"

I put the book down and sighed. "It's like astrology. There's this legend that says the Buddha called all the animals together to say good-bye to him when he was about to leave the earth, but only twelve showed up, so he named a year after each of them."

"What's that got to do with you?" Pig asked.

"If you were born in the year of the rat, say, then you're supposed to have a personality similar to that animal's. That's what I am: a rat."

"Cool," Pig said. "Look me up in there."

"Okay, when were you born? I have to know the date. The Chinese calendar is different from ours because it's based on lunar cycles."

"December twenty-fourth. I was the Pighetti family's Christmas present."

"Let's see," I said, flipping back to the table of lunar years at the front of the book. "That makes you a . . . wow! This is incredible!"

"What?" Pig said.

"This stuff really works," I said, my voice quavering.

"What is it? What am I?" Pig asked, craning his neck to look over the top of the book.

I looked him right in the eye. "You're a boar," I said. "A wild pig."

"Hmmm," he said, pursing his lips. "Wild pig. I like the sound of that. It's better than being a plain old barnyard pig." He put two fingers up to make tusks, then started grunting and running circles around me. Then he stopped and did a little dance and sang, "Wild pig. Doo-doo, doo doo doo doo. You make my heart sing."

"All right, all right. Settle down. Don't you want to hear what you're like?"

"Sure. Go ahead. I'll tell you if you're right."

" 'The Boar is the sign of simplicity, honesty and great fortitude,' " I read. " 'Gallant, chivalrous, sturdy and courageous . . . he may appear rough-hewn and jovial, but scratch the surface and you will find pure gold.' "

Pig swelled his chest with pride. "Yup, that's me. Read on."

" 'The original nice guy . . . he seeks universal harmony. He is thick-skinned and can dismiss insults and unpleasantries with a shrug. No doubt he will have fights and differences with others, but he will not carry grudges unless you give him no choice . . . then he may respond savagely and turn into a raging foe. He is the kind of person we tend to take for granted until he leaves us to fend for ourselves.' "

"Don't I have any bad qualities?"

"I'm getting to that," I said. " 'The Boar is equally known for his hefty appetite and wanton pursuit of pleasure. His main fault will be his inability to say "No" firmly to himself, his family and his friends. Most of the Boar's problems stem from his overgenerous nature.' "

"How do you like that? My only fault is I'm too nice."

"Don't forget the hefty appetite part," I said, closing the book. "And speaking of that, how's your food diary coming along?"

"Great. Writing down what I eat is almost as much fun as eating it. I've almost filled this one," he said, taking the notebook out of his pocket and flapping it in front of me.

"What about your fat grams?"

"I don't know," Pig said. "I lost the fat counter you gave me."

"Lost it!" I said, slapping my forehead. "Then how do you know what to eat?"

"I have an instinct for these things," Pig said.

"Your instincts had better be sharper than they were last week. Or I'll have a lot of explaining to do when I see Ms. Bodine. Maybe you and your notebook should come over to my place tomorrow night so I can total up your fat grams. Besides, it will give me a chance to tell you about the next phase of your diet."

"What are you talking about? I thought we were almost finished."

"We're almost finished doing low-fat," I said. "But we still have to do the low-fat, high-fiber program, and then finish up with low-fat and exercise."

"Fiber! Exercise!" Pig said, like a lookout who had just spotted the enemy.

I unzipped the outside pocket of my backpack and rummaged around until I found a blank notebook and handed it to him. "That's right, and it will all be recorded in here: 'The Diary of Angelo Pighetti, Volume Two.' "

"I hope it isn't a horror story," Pig moaned.

CHAPTER 13

My mom and I were sitting in the living room when the doorbell rang, and she went to answer it.

"You must be Angelo Pighetti. I'm Tucker's mom, Andrea Harrison."

"Nice to meet you," Pig said. "Tucker asked me to come over. We're working on a school project together."

"Yes, I know. He told me about you. You're the friend whose family owns the pizza place. Tucker's in the living room waiting for you," she said as she closed the door behind him. "Would you like to sit down?"

I jumped off the sofa before he could answer. "We've got to get to work," I said, "after we have our snack."

I went into the hallway and Pig followed, still looking back over his shoulder at the living room.

"Your mom's cool, Tucker," he said as we walked into the kitchen. "She doesn't seem at all like a shrink."

"Who says shrinks can't be cool?" I asked.

101

"I didn't mean that. It's just that I thought they were all old and had beards."

"She only wears her beard to the office," I said.

I pulled a plate out of the refrigerator, slipped it in the microwave and pushed some buttons. "Are you ready for some grub?" I asked.

"What is it?" Pig asked, peering over my shoulder.

"My newest invention: high-fiber pasta. All you have to do is eat a plate of this every morning for the next week. It will give you all the fiber you need each day for the next phase of your diet: fifty grams per serving."

Pig's expression soured as I set the plate down in front of him. "Did you say grub—or grubs?" he asked.

I pulled open a drawer and handed him a knife and fork. "Grub. I said *grub*. Here, dig in."

He held the knife and fork up on either side of the plate and stared at it. "No offense, Tucker, but that's the fattest, ugliest spaghetti I've ever seen. It looks like a pile of huge maggots."

"I had to roll it out by hand," I said, pantomiming. "You know, the way you did with clay in preschool. I tried using the pasta machine, but it kept getting clogged up and I couldn't clean it. My mom's going to kill me when she sees it. I sure hope she doesn't have a craving for fettuccine Alfredo anytime soon."

Pig pushed his fork into the center and twirled it around; then he stuck a big wad of pasta in his mouth and began to chew. Suddenly he stopped. His eyes bugged out. I knew he was in trouble because he began frantically waving his hands and pointing at his mouth.

He tried to speak but all that came out were desperate grunts. I reached over and squeezed his cheeks together, but it didn't do any good. I kept thinking about the pasta machine and wondering how long it took for this stuff to harden. Desperately I stuck my fingers in his mouth and pulled his teeth apart with a loud sucking sound. Pig went running to the sink to spit the whole thing down the garbage disposal.

"What's in that stuff?" he said, wiping his mouth with a napkin. "It's dangerous."

"Flour, eggs, ground barley, oat bran . . ."

"Oat bran and ground barley? Why don't you throw in a little sawdust? Or maybe some pencil shavings?"

I poked at the pile of noodles with the fork.

"It probably just needs more water to make it less chewy," I said.

"It's not chewy, Tucker. Cement mix is not chewy. Even a goat couldn't digest this stuff. I'm not eating another bite of it. Take my advice. Stick with science. Leave cooking to the experts."

I scraped the plate in the sink, flipped on the disposal and watched my invention disappear in a noisy swirl down the drain.

"Guess we'll just have to figure out another way to get fiber in your diet."

"Yeah, maybe I could eat old shoes."

I walked out of the kitchen and Pig slumped after me. "I wonder if this is how Dr. Frankenstein got started," he muttered, trailing me up the stairs.

When we got to my room, Pig flung himself down on

my bed and I sat down at my desk in front of the computer.

"Did you bring your food diary?" I asked.

Pig rolled over and pulled it out of his back pocket.

"Here," he said, flinging it through the air in my general direction. "Read it and weep."

I flipped through the first half of the notebook, then read one of the pages out loud:

Wednesday, October 9

3:00 P.M.   One slice pepperoni pizza.

3:30 P.M.   The pizza made me thirsty. Two glasses of juice, and some Italian bread.

3:45 P.M.   Leftovers from the deli case. My mom asked me to clean it out.

4:15 P.M.   One Italian sub that José accidentally made for a lady who said she'd ordered tuna.

4:30 P.M.   A whole lot of fruit and some salad.

5:00 P.M.   Two pieces of the cake Papa made for Louie's birthday. He made it in the shape of a bird. I had a wing and a leg. Louie wouldn't eat any. He's a vegetarian.

"All of this between three and five o'clock?" I asked. "How can you expect to lose any weight like this?"

Pig looked hurt.

"I was trying to eat the food triangle . . . just like you said."

"I guess I didn't expect your triangle to be this big. Plus, it's upside down. The bad foods are the fat part of the triangle, and the good foods are the tip. Well, at least we know what some of the problems are. Now let's check your weight."

I went into the bathroom and came back with the scale.

"Okay," I said, setting it down next to him. "Step on it."

"No thanks," he said, folding his hands behind his head. "I'm comfortable right here on the bed."

"Come on, Pig."

He stepped on the scale and tried to look over his stomach at the numbers in front of his feet. "Well, how did I do?" he asked.

"One hundred and eighty-two big ones," I said, writing it down in my notebook. "Great, just great. Two weeks under my careful scrutiny and you've gained two pounds."

Pig pretended to be alarmed. "Good grief," he gasped. "We'd better give up before I get any fatter."

"You're right," I said, "giving up is a great idea . . ."

He looked at me suspiciously.

". . . and you can start by giving up lunch meat and dessert."

I threw my notebook on the desk and sank down in a heap on my bed. "This project is a disaster. There's got to be a way to get you to eat healthy foods."

"Like how?"

"I don't know. I'll have to think about it."

"Good. You think, and I'll do something else. Got any good computer games?"

"They're all in this file," I said. I went to the desk and pulled out a CD-ROM, stuck it in the computer and turned it on. "Try this one. It's brand new. I read about it in *Macworld* and ordered it through the mail."

Pig picked up the empty box and read the front.

" 'Virtual World. The game that's more real than your life . . . and a whole lot more fun.' "

He scanned the pictures, then flipped over the box and read the back. " 'Journey beyond the boundaries of space and time. Visit an uncharted island. Explore the undersea realm. Discover fortresses hidden in mysterious jungles. Conquer raging rivers and high mountain peaks. But watch your step. Danger awaits you at every turn.' "

I got up from my chair and let Pig sit down in front of the computer while I flopped down on my stomach on the bed.

"Hey, this is cool, Tucker."

He clicked the mouse button and brought up a picture of a dark staircase leading down to a wharf with an empty rowboat quietly bobbing on the water.

"Look at these stunningly realistic 3-D graphics. Don't you love the original sound effects and the incredible animation?"

"You sound just like the box," I said, propping up my chin with my fists while I watched him move the mouse around to explore the wharf.

"I know. That's where I got it. How do you get out to that island?"

"Well, I'd say you can either swim or use the boat. I'd take the boat if I were you. I fell off the dock the last time I played, and there were piranhas in the water."

Pig clicked on the boat.

"Why isn't it moving?"

"You forgot to untie it."

"Oh yeah."

He clicked on the ropes that held the boat to the dock and they fell slack in the water. The boat started to drift away from the dock.

"Hey. How do you control this thing? Isn't there a steering wheel or something?"

"It's a rowboat," I said. "You left the oars on the dock."

"What am I going to do now?" he asked.

"Guess you'll just have to drift with the current."

Pig was fidgeting a little as he watched his boat drift downstream.

"I think we're going faster," he said, sounding a little concerned. "Maybe I should try to grab one of those tree branches that are hanging out over the bank."

"Okay. But remember, if you fall in, you're fish food."

"Darn, I missed. Boy, these *are* stunningly realistic graphics. I feel like the boat's rocking each time we get hit by one of those waves."

There was a loud *thunk* from the computer.

"What was that?" Pig said, holding on to the edge of the desk to steady himself.

"I think you hit a rock, or maybe you were attacked by an unusually large and hungry piranha."

"Oh my gosh. It must have been a rock. There's water coming in the bottom of my boat," Pig said, beginning to panic.

"Click on the bucket up front and start to bail," I advised him.

"It's coming in faster than I can empty it out," he said, panting for breath even though the computer was doing all the work. "I've got to find a way out of here. I'm virtually terrified. Hey, what's that up ahead?"

"Uh-oh," I said, shaking my head. "I think it's the waterfall."

"What? No!"

Pig dropped the mouse, closed his eyes and held on to the chair arms so tightly his knuckles turned white.

"Help me, Tucker. I'm going to be virtual history."

I jumped off the bed, grabbed the mouse button and clicked the castle icon. The scene changed to a picture of a drawbridge leading across a moat to a pair of large wooden doors.

Pig peeked at the screen through one eye, then took the mouse from me. "Whoooo! Thanks. That was close."

He clicked on the door and it creaked open. A soldier holding a large spear across the opening appeared on the screen. "Halt. Who goes there?" the soldier bellowed.

"It's me, Angelo Pighetti, Your Royal Guardness."

"He can't hear you," I said. "You have to type it in."

Pig typed in his name, and a message appeared on the screen: "Password not accepted."

"You'll have to create a new password," I said. I erased his name and typed in "Sir Angelo the Portly and his loyal companion, Friar Tuck."

"Enter, Sir Portly and Friar Tuck," the soldier said, shouldering his spear. "The king awaits you in his chamber."

"Wow, look at this," Pig said as a picture of the grand entry hall appeared on the screen. "The king must have robbed a lot of peasants to pay for this place."

Pig moved the mouse around the hallway until he found another guard standing at the staircase. Then he typed in "Which way is the dining room?"

"What are you doing? We're supposed to go to the king's chambers."

"I know, but I'm getting hungry. I thought maybe we could talk one of the scullery maids into giving us a little virtual food."

He entered his question and several more guards came out of nowhere and surrounded us with their swords drawn.

"Oh-oh. I think I said something wrong."

"No, wait, I think that's the answer," I said.

"The answer to what, how we can get our heads chopped off? These guys don't look like a welcoming party."

"Not the game. My science fair project."

"Huh?"

I switched off the computer.

"Hey, what did you do that for? I could have fought my way out of it. If I can handle Jonah, I can handle a few knights with swords. Whop, chop, chop, heeeeaahh," Pig said, pantomiming a karate fight with the knights.

"Quit goofing around," I said. "This is important. I know how I can help you lose weight now."

"You do?"

"Yup. You just gave me the answer."

"I did? I didn't mean to."

"Two words. Virtual food."

"You want me to have dinner with a computer each night? What are you going to do, show me pictures of stunningly realistic 3-D pizzas while I sit here and drool?"

"Not exactly. I'm just going to take advantage of your amazingly vivid, state-of-the-art imagination. From now on, you can eat the foods that are good for you, but when it comes to second helpings, desserts, chips and greasy stuff like pepperoni and salami—I want you to just pretend to eat it. You can look at it, you can sniff it, you can dream about how it would taste if you were rolling it around on your tongue. The only thing you can't do is put it in your mouth."

"You want me to eat healthy food and then pig out in my imagination?"

"Exactly."

Pig just shook his head and rolled his eyes.

"This isn't going to work, Tucker."

"How do you know until you try?"

"I may not know science the way you do, but I'm an expert on Angelo Pighetti."

"Maybe you'll find out something about yourself you didn't know."

"That," he said, "is exactly what I'm afraid of."

CHAPTER 14

Before class the next morning, Pig told me he was going to have to work at the restaurant most of the week after school. They were shorthanded because José Sanchez, the guy who worked behind the deli counter and waited tables, had disappeared. No one knew exactly what had happened because Mrs. Sanchez only spoke Spanish and they hadn't found anyone to translate yet. The only thing she said that anyone understood was "I.N.S."

I volunteered to help out too. I told myself it was a good way to keep Pig under surveillance. But the truth was, I liked it there. Frankie's Pizza was noisy, messy and out of control, but so was my life at this point.

The people at the restaurant yelled at each other, but they also laughed a lot. It was never boring like my house. And there was always music at Pig's house. Mr. Pighetti loved opera. When he wasn't shouting at people or kissing them, he was usually singing along with *La Traviata* or *Rigoletto*. He sang in Italian, but sometimes he'd tell us the stories in English. I was learning a lot about love, death, murder and betrayal, which seemed to be mostly what opera was about.

What I wasn't learning much about was how to help Pig lose weight. As the week wore on, it was becoming clear to me that I should have listened when he told me he knew Angelo Pighetti better than I did. Between the food diary, virtual food, and the restaurant, he was spending most of his waking hours either writing about, thinking about, making, serving or eating food. It was an explosive situation, and by the following Thursday afternoon the fuse was getting pretty short.

"How come Angelo has his head in the oven?" Mrs. Pighetti asked after school that day.

"He said he wanted to smell the pepperoni pizza," Mr. Pighetti said as he spread tomato sauce on several crusts with a spoon.

Pig was standing in front of the oven with his eyes closed, holding the door open and taking deep breaths though his nose, then exhaling with a loud "haaaaaaa" sound through his mouth.

"Enough," Mr. Pighetti said. "If you do that much longer you're going to pass out. Here," he said, handing Pig a white Styrofoam takeout box. "Bring this to the register, and hurry it up. I'd hate to see a customer starve to death while he's waiting for his food. It's bad for business."

"What's in it?" Pig asked.

"Cannoli."

"Could I look at it?"

"Why? You don't believe me?"

"I just want to look, okay? Mmmm," Pig said, prying off the top. "I love those little green nuts on the end and that sweet creamy filling, and the crust is so crisp with just a little bit of powdered sugar sprinkled on the outside."

Mr. Pighetti took the box and closed it up again.

"Angelo! You're going to drool on the cannoli."

Mrs. Pighetti smiled and shook her head, then steered Pig back through the kitchen door.

"Maybe it's the fumes from the oven," Mr. Pighetti said to me, tapping his head with his finger. "Yesterday he told me we ought to switch to whole-wheat spaghetti. I asked him what was so great about it, and you know what he said to me? 'It's got fiber, Papa.' Fiber! What's going on with that kid?"

Mr. Pighetti took some broccoli and green pepper out of the cooler and set them down in a pile in front of me

"Chop these up for me, will you, Tucker?" he asked. "I'm starting to run out. Everybody wants the vegetarian pizza today. What's the matter with meat?"

Pig walked back through the door.

"Hey, Angelo," Mr. Pighetti said, reaching up to take a plate from under the warming lamp. "Bring this sausage to Vinnie Venuti. Now there's a guy who'll never put the butchers out of business."

Pig took the plate and sniffed the air above it.

"Ahhhh. The sauce smells great today," Pig said. "Lots of oregano. But I think you used a little too much basil."

113

"What are you, a restaurant critic? Stop sniffing the food and bring it to the customer," Mr. Pighetti said.

Pig kept moving his nose closer and closer to the sausage. I was afraid he was going to stick his face in it.

"I'd better help him," I said, taking my apron off. "I can chop those vegetables when I get back."

Mr. Pighetti shrugged and threw his hands in the air.

"Whatever Angelo's got must be catching," he called after us. "Now you're both acting crazy."

It was late afternoon, and the tables were starting to fill up as the dinner crowd arrived.

"Which one's Venuti?" I asked Pig.

"That big guy at the table next to Mr. Kleinkopf. The one that looks like a weight lifter. Actually he's a cop. My dad used to live down the street from him. He told me when he was a little kid, Vinnie was smaller than everybody, so everyone picked on him. Then he grew up and got even."

Pig took one last whiff of the Italian sausage.

"Boy, this stuff smells good today," he said.

"Here's your dinner, Mr. Venuti," Pig said.

He held it out to him, but when Officer Venuti reached up to take it, Pig wouldn't let go. It was as though his fingers were glued to the plate. Every time Officer Venuti pulled the plate down toward the table, Pig pulled it back again. They kept going back and forth, back and forth in a kind of tug-of-war, until finally I took it away from both of them and set it down.

"Come on, Angelo," I said, pulling at his sleeve. "We have to get back to work, right?"

"Hold it," Mr. Kleinkopf said, leaning over from his table. "Maybe there's a reason Angelo doesn't want to set the plate down. Maybe he knows something."

Mr. Kleinkopf turned his watery brown eyes on me. "That kid tried to poison me a few days ago," he said.

Officer Venuti stuck out his lips. "That the truth, kid?"

I backed away a few steps and opened my mouth, but nothing came out.

"There's nothing wrong with your sausage, Mr. Venuti," Pig said. "Honest. I'll even prove it."

Pig picked up a fork, stabbed a big hunk of sausage and stuck it in his mouth.

"See," he said, the partially chewed sausage bulging out his cheeks. "It's harmless."

He smiled first at Officer Venuti, then at Mr. Kleinkopf, then at me, as he gulped it down.

"That was really good," he said, his eyes sparkling. He lifted his fork to stab another hunk. I tried to grab it out of his hand, but Mr. Kleinkopf waved me off.

"No! Let him have more. There's no reason he shouldn't . . . is there, kid?" he asked, squinting at me.

"I . . . I guess not," I said, "except maybe I should be the one to eat this bite . . . just to prove everything's all right."

I slipped the fork out of his hand, stabbed a bite of sausage and ate it.

Pig glared at me.

"I can handle this," he said, seizing the fork and wolfing down a few more bites.

Officer Venuti stood up, nearly knocking over his chair.

I was afraid he was going for his gun, but he grabbed the fork out of Pig's hand instead.

"Okay, okay. There's nothing wrong with the sausage," he said, waving us off. "You can go now. I'll just eat whatever's left."

"Sorry, Mr. Venuti," Pig said. "I don't know what came over me. I'll go get you some garlic bread."

We went into the kitchen together, and I picked up the knife to finish chopping vegetables while Pig filled a basket with bread.

"You've got to stop doing this, Pig. All you've done all afternoon is talk about food, smell food and look at food. You're only making it harder for yourself."

"But I'm only doing what you told me to do. Imagining what it would be like to eat anything I want. It all seems so real," he said, picking up a slice of warm garlic bread and holding it up to the light. "It's almost like I'm really eating it. Like I'm sitting down at one of those tables out there and it's just covered with all the foods I like and it's not just in my mind."

As he spoke, the garlic bread was moving closer to his mouth. I was starting to get nervous and began to chop faster and faster.

"I pick one out and lift it slowly, like this. Taking time to really appreciate it. Then I open my mouth and. . . ."

"Ow!" I yelled. Blood squirted out of my finger. I stuck it in my mouth, then went to the sink and held it under cold water. Pig brought me a Band-Aid.

"Did you chop it bad?" he asked.

"Not as bad as I chopped the broccoli."

Pig opened the Band-Aid and wrapped it around my finger. Mrs. Pighetti came in and picked up the garlic bread Pig had been working on.

"Who's this for?" she asked.

"Mr. Venuti."

Before we could stop her, she walked back out the door.

"I wonder what he's going to say when he realizes there's a bite out of it?" Pig said.

Suddenly we heard loud voices coming from the restaurant.

"Whoa! He's *really* mad," Pig said. We rushed through the door into the restaurant, expecting Officer Venuti to be hauling Mrs. Pighetti in for serving him half-eaten garlic bread. But instead we found Mrs. Sanchez, who was very pregnant, screaming and crying. Mrs. Pighetti had her arm around her and was saying something soothing to her in Italian.

"What is it?" I asked Pig. "Is she going to deliver the baby?"

"I don't know. The only words I understood were 'landlord' and *'morta'*. That means 'dead.'"

"Do you think we should call nine-one-one?" I asked.

"Not if he's already dead," Pig said.

"Why is your mom talking to her in Italian?"

Pig shrugged. "It's the only other language she knows."

Mrs. Sanchez pulled Mama Pighetti out the front door, and everyone in Frankie's Pizza, including the customers, poured out into the street to see what was happening, except for Mr. Kleinkopf, who hid under the table.

117

When I looked across the street, I saw what the problem was. Mrs. Sanchez's landlord wasn't dead. She only wished he was dead. She had been evicted. Everything she owned—her furniture, her clothes, her food, her children's toys—had been dumped in a huge pile at the curb.

Mrs. Pighetti was hugging Mrs. Sanchez, who was still crying and now had several small children with her, crying and holding on to her skirt. Mr. Pighetti went across the street to talk to the two men who were carrying the last of Mrs. Sanchez's belongings out of her apartment. I couldn't hear what they were saying, but there was a lot of shouting and gesturing. Then the two men went out to the curb and started carrying everything across the street to the restaurant.

Angelo came out to watch the men bringing armloads of clothes and toys into Frankie's Pizza.

"Looks like Mrs. Sanchez is moving in again," he said to me.

"Again? You mean they've done this before?"

Pig nodded.

"When they first came from Mexico and my dad gave José his job, they lived with us for two months."

"Your family's amazing, Pig. I can't imagine my dad . . . or even my mom . . . letting a bunch of strangers move in. We have a hard enough time living with our relatives."

"Mrs. Sanchez isn't a stranger. She's our friend."

"But she doesn't even speak the same language you do."

"Who says friends have to speak the same language?"

"Well, it might help if you could understand each other."

"We do understand each other . . . well enough to help."

"Yeah." I nodded, watching Mrs. Pighetti scoop up one of the Sanchez children in each of her arms. "I guess you're right."

CHAPTER 15

Sunday night I began to panic. My next meeting with Ms. Bodine was looming on the horizon. There were only ten days left until my final report was due, and so far all my results fell into two categories: bad and worse. If virtual food turned out to be a flop like everything else I had tried, I was going down with it.

I'd asked Pig to meet me at the nurse's office on Monday morning so I could weigh him, since he was too busy working at the restaurant now to come to my house after school. The nurse's scale was probably more reliable and scientific than mine was anyway. The only problem was that to use it, I had to first get rid of the nurse.

"Come on in," I said when Pig showed up. "The coast is clear."

"Where's Mrs. Schroenhamer?" he asked.

"I told her there was an outbreak of head lice in Mr. Dolton's classroom and she should get down there right away and do head checks."

"What happens if she doesn't find any?"

"Then I'll congratulate her on averting another disaster. Besides, maybe she will find some. Then she can congratulate me."

Pig set down his books and stepped on the scale, then slid the weights to the center of the bar.

"You've gained another two pounds!" I nearly shouted at him.

"I can't help it. Ever since you told me about virtual food, it's all I think about. And when I think about food, I want to eat it."

"Stop thinking about it, then."

"It's not that easy. It's like I'm hypnotized."

"Then I guess I'm going to have to find a way to un-hypnotize you. Listen, I've got to go. I'm already late for a meeting about my project. Just meet me in the lunchroom at noon . . . and don't eat anything until I get there."

I raced down the hall to Ms. Bodine's office, nearly running into one of the custodians, who was coming out of the bathroom pushing a bucket of water on wheels. Although I managed not to fall in, as I veered out of the way I knocked the mop out of the bucket. When I tried to set it back up again, some of the water slopped over the sides.

"Sorry," I muttered, thinking the janitor would be mad and make me clean it up. But instead he smiled and put his hand on my shoulder.

"Hey, slow down, kid," he said. "You're too young for pressure."

When I reached the outer office, I stopped long enough

to realize the secretary was away from her desk, then burst through the open door of Ms. Bodine's room. "I didn't mean to be late, but . . . ," I panted. Then I realized we weren't alone.

"It's all right, Tucker," Ms. Bodine reassured me. "Beth Ellen and I were just finishing our conference. You probably know by now that Tucker's our other entrant for the science fair," she said to Beth Ellen as I sat down in the chair next to her. "Did he tell you his project is on nutrition and obesity?"

"Yes, but that's *all* I know so far," Beth Ellen said.

"Perhaps you'd like to stay and hear more about it." Ms. Bodine smiled.

"Oh, I don't think she'd find my project very interesting," I blurted out, digging both of my fists into my chair.

Beth Ellen raised one eyebrow as she glanced at me.

"Don't be so modest," she said, crossing her legs and settling back into her chair. "I'd love to find out more about Tucker's project."

"Well, then," Ms. Bodine said, "tell us how the low-fat portion of the diet's been going. Did Angelo lose any weight?"

Beth Ellen's mouth dropped open and she glared at me. I leaned over and slid the graph I'd made across Ms. Bodine's desk, and she studied the horizontal line.

"I didn't get any dramatic results with that program," I said. "As a matter of fact, I haven't gotten any results at all."

"What about the low-fat, high-fiber diet?" Ms. Bodine asked.

Beth Ellen had painted purple flowers on her long green nails and she was clicking them on the arm of her chair, making it difficult for me to concentrate.

"I don't have the results entered yet, but I expect them to be more . . . significant."

Ms. Bodine flipped through the rest of the stack of papers. "Well, it looks like everything's on schedule. We'll just have to wait and see what results you obtain. Don't forget, you'll need to make transparencies of your graphs for the overhead projector. Beth Ellen, do you have anything to add?"

She swiveled around to face Ms. Bodine. "I know this isn't my call . . . but . . . well, I still have to tell you what I think." Beth Ellen shifted in her chair and looked directly at me. "I don't like Tucker using Angelo as his experiment."

Ms. Bodine pressed her hands together and rested her fingertips on her lips. "Yes," she said finally. "I fully appreciate your concern, Beth Ellen. In fact, Tucker and I talked this over at the beginning of the project. So long as the diet's a healthy one and Angelo wants to participate, I think everything will be fine." She stood up and pushed her chair back. "I'm afraid I have another student waiting to meet with me on another matter. All results will need to be in by a week from Wednesday, so I'll expect one more progress report from each of you. Keep up the good work."

Beth Ellen was quiet until we were out in the hall, and then she grabbed my arm.

"I don't know what you're up to, but I've got a bad

123

feeling about it. I can't believe Angelo's doing this because he wants to, and I don't even want to think about how you talked him into it. You'd better not do anything to hurt him, Tucker."

"How can I possibly hurt him by helping him lose weight? He's fat, Beth Ellen. He's five four and he weighs one hundred eighty-five pounds."

Beth Ellen's eyes flashed with anger. "People are just numbers to you, aren't they? Height, weight, IQ, class rank. If you can't weigh it measure it or score it, it isn't real. That's how you think, isn't it, Tucker?"

"I only want to teach him something that will make his life better."

"He should be teaching you, Tucker. You may be a genius at science, but Angelo's a genius at the things that really matter."

There was a long pause before she spoke again.

"And you don't even know what they are."

Pig was leaning against the brick wall outside the lunchroom when I caught up with him at noon that day. "Did you get the sandwich I left in your locker?" I asked.

"I got it all right, but I don't have it anymore."

I stopped and stared at him. "What?"

"I gave it to Jonah." Pig shrugged. "He said if I didn't give it to him he was going to see if pigs really squeal when you stick them or if they just say *oink*."

I threw my arms up in the air. I felt like I wanted to hit someone but I wasn't sure who. "That was a valuable sandwich. There were at least twenty grams of fiber in it. You shouldn't have turned it over to him without a fight."

"A fight?" Pig wrinkled up his face in disbelief. "Oh, sure. I suppose if you had been there you would have defended my lunch to the death. There were three of them and there was only one of me."

I wheeled around to face him.

"Jonah's a coward, Pig. That's why there's three of them. Hyenas always travel in packs. Only it's just a small pack because he could only find two friends stupid enough to follow him. If you ever once stood up to him . . ."

I noticed Pig staring past me at something behind my back with a worried look on his face, and I stopped talking.

"He's standing behind me, isn't he?" I asked quietly.

Pig nodded.

"And he's not alone, is he?"

Pig shook his head. I turned around and there was Jonah smiling down at me, while Brian Woomer and another guy sneered over his shoulder.

"Don't stop now," Jonah said. "It was just starting to get interesting. Tell us the part about the hyenas again. We're a little stupid. We might have to hear it twice."

He put a hand on my shoulder and pushed his thumb into the bone so hard that I winced and tried to break away from his grip.

"Better yet, just stand there and shut up," Jonah said, shoving me aside.

He turned to face Pig.

"You're the one I want to talk to. About that little trick you played on me."

Pig just stared at him.

"I don't think Pig gets it, Jonah," one of his friends said. "Maybe he doesn't speak your language."

"Oh, I'm sorry." Jonah needled him. "How about *ig-pay atin-lay*? You understand that, fat boy?" Pig bit his lip and scowled at him.

"I already gave you my lunch."

"You mean this lunch?" Jonah asked, shoving a brown paper bag into Pig's chest.

Jonah pulled some sprouts out of the bag, held them up in front of Pig's face, then dropped them at his feet.

"You don't eat this stuff. Where's your real lunch?"

"That's it," Pig said.

"Well, it better go back to being pizza by tomorrow, or I'm going to have to make ground pork out of you. Got it?"

Jonah punched his fist into his hand as he and his friends bulldozed past us.

"I'll see you later, Shrink, so we can have that little talk about hyenas," he said.

Pig and I stood there with our heads hanging and our shoulders slumped, waiting until they got out of earshot.

"I'm dead meat," I said.

"Yeah," Pig moaned, "and I'm Italian sausage."

CHAPTER 16

I couldn't take the bus home because I knew Jonah would be on it. If I walked home instead there was a good chance I'd run into Brian Woomer, known to his victims as Boomer Woomer, at least to those who could still speak. So I went to Pig's house after school. I knew I'd be safe there . . . for a while, at least. But sooner or later I would have to walk home.

When we finished our snack after school that day, Mrs. Pighetti put us to work cutting green peppers in the kitchen. We were both quiet for a long time. All you could hear was the *chop, chop, chop* of the knife hitting the board.

"Are you worried about Jonah, like I am?" I asked to break the uncomfortable silence.

Pig nodded. "Boomer doesn't bother me too much. He just likes to hit things. That's why he plays the drums in the school band. He told me so himself. But Jonah's different. He likes to hurt things. He's plain mean."

I thought about the difference awhile.

"Have you ever actually been beaten up by anyone?" I asked, wanting and not wanting to know what it was like.

"Yeah," Pig said. "A few times. But I never got hurt, 'cause of what my dad's cousin taught me. Vincenzo Pighetti. He's sort of a legend in our family. The one guy that really made good."

"What is he, a prizefighter?"

Pig shook his head. "Nope. A tenor. He came to stay with us one year when he was starring at the summer festival theater."

"So what does an opera star know about fighting?" I asked, scraping the chopped peppers into a pile and picking another pepper out of the basket.

"He knows about stage fighting," Pig said. "He took a class in it at the Lyric Opera. Once he had to do a sixty-second sword fight and they spent two weeks rehearsing it with this guy from Hollywood. You had to know just where to stand each second or your head would be rolling across the stage."

Pig whacked a big green pepper with his knife to illustrate, splitting it open so little white seeds came flying out.

"I thought they used rubber swords," I said, sliding my cutting board a little farther away from Pig's.

"Uh-uh. They use real broadswords. Big ones. The audience likes to hear them clink. It's sort of like a dance . . . a dangerous dance."

"I don't get how that helps you if the other guy doesn't know you're dancing."

"Put down your knife and I'll show you."

Pig grabbed my shoulders and spun me around. Then he faced me with his arms hanging at his sides. "If someone's going to hit you, you don't try to defend yourself. Just stand there. Watch their eyes. Watch their fists. And when you see one flying at you, you jump back and pretend you got hit. Go ahead," he said, pointing to his nose. "Hit me here. Go on. Do it."

I hesitated for a moment, then took a swing at him. Just as my fist brushed his cheek, he slapped his thigh and threw his head back, howling in pain.

"If he hits you in the face, you fall on the ground and pretend to be unconscious and the guy is so busy thinking about how strong he is that he doesn't hit you again. And if he hits you in the gut, you fly back like this," he said, staggering backward and crashing down on the kitchen floor. "Then you lie there, clutching your stomach and kicking your legs, yelling 'Ow! Oooh! You hit me too hard. I think you ruptured something. Call a doctor.' "

Just at that moment Mrs. Pighetti burst through the kitchen door.

"Angelo!" she shouted down at him. "Tucker, what have you done? What's the matter with you boys, fighting like this?" She rushed to Pig's side and bent over him. "Where does it hurt, *bambino*?"

Pig stopped writhing and boosted himself up on his elbows. "Nowhere, Mama. We were just playing."

The concerned look disappeared from Mrs. Pighetti's face and was replaced by fury. "Playing? In my kitchen? When you're supposed to be chopping green peppers?"

"Sorry, Mama." Pig got to his feet and offered his mother a hand up, then steered her to a chair in the corner. "Why don't you sit down and rest awhile? Tucker and I will take your orders out for you."

We gathered up the plates and walked toward the door. "Next time," Pig whispered, "I'll show you how they do it with swords."

I decided to wait until it was almost dark to walk home, and I called Mrs. Hrabik to let her know I'd be late. She seemed a little nervous about the idea.

"Wait there," she commanded. "Mommy pick you up. Not now. After work."

"It's no big deal," I said. "I'm not a baby. I can walk."

Once I was on my way, I started wishing I'd listened to her. I thought it would be harder for Jonah to see me in the dark, but I forgot that it would also be harder for me to see him. I kept looking over my shoulder, thinking I heard footsteps, but there was never anyone there. Every time I came to an alley, I stopped and waited to see if anyone was going to leap out of the shadows and grab me before I rushed on.

I even took a different way home, hoping to avoid Jonah. But it backfired on me. I had gone a roundabout way, thinking I knew where to turn, and I ended up on a street I'd never seen before. It was in a dingy neighborhood with littered streets lit by neon lights, and dirty buildings plastered with handbills. A lot of the storefronts were empty, and the rest seemed to be either junk shops, bars or the kind of run-down grocery stores that sold a lot more cigarettes and lottery tickets than food.

I was afraid I'd get even more lost if I turned back. So I decided to stop and ask directions at a gas station.

"Where you want to go, kid?" the station attendant asked me from his glass booth. His dark hair was pulled back into a ponytail, and he had tattoos on both arms.

"Riverwood Drive. Six hundred," I said.

"Man, you are one long way from home." He whistled softly through his teeth. "You go north over the tracks," he said, stretching his arm out to point the way. "Go three blocks, then turn east on Fairview. The next stoplight, you turn left. That's Humboldt. Keep following that and you're home free."

I had to wait for what seemed like forever while a freight train went by. At first I was standing under the streetlight, but when I realized how easy it would be to spot me there, I moved into the shadows and waited, watching the tank cars and flatcars lumber by, clicking and screeching as they went. As soon as the caboose went past, I ran across the tracks before the lights had even stopped flashing and the gates were fully up.

When I got to Fairview, I had to stop and think about which way east was. Hopelessly confused, I stepped into the street and nearly got killed when a car squealed around the corner, blasting me with its horn. I turned right, but when I saw the factories and empty parking lots that lined the street, I started to worry that I'd gotten lost again.

Finally I came to the stoplight and turned left on Humboldt. It was even darker and more deserted than Fairview. To build up my courage, I began to practice doing Pig's self-defense dance. I passed a darkened doorway and imagined Jonah reaching out to pull me in; then I spun around and escaped him. I pretended he tried to punch me and I leaped into the air so he missed. I imagined Boomer coming out of nowhere, and I whirled around to face him. "If you want to hit something, hit your drums," I shouted at the imaginary Boomer. Then I kicked the air ferociously.

I was starting to really enjoy Pig's dangerous dance. It made me feel strong, going down the street that way. I was leaping. I was spinning. I was whirling. Then I heard someone calling to me from across the street. There was a group of guys, standing in front of a hot dog stand, hooting at me.

"Hey, you," someone shouted. "You forgot your tutu." Two guys started to walk across the street toward me. My heart thumped in my chest. Some of their friends straggled after them.

"Maybe he's wearing it under his pants," a tall guy said, stepping up and spinning me around by the shoulders. "They look kind of fluffy in the back."

His friends laughed and stepped closer, forming a circle around me.

"You're lucky you ran into us tonight," the tall guy said. "It just so happens Mike here gives ballet lessons to aspiring dancers like yourself."

"Yeah," Mike said, sneering at me. "But they don't come cheap."

"I . . . I don't have any money on me," I said. I backed away from him and bumped into the guy standing behind me.

"No money?" He shook his head. "I guess you'll have to apply for a scholarship, then. Tell you what. Do that twirl again for me, and I'll let you know whether or not you're worth my time."

I looked around. The street was empty except for a man leaning against a building, asleep. I decided I'd better go along with their joke and started spinning.

"Put your hands up, like this," Mike said. He lifted my arms up over my head. I twirled around again and his friends burst out laughing.

"Now, get up on your toes. Come on, you can do it." He pulled me up by the wrists and I whirled around on tiptoes with my arms in the air. They were laughing so hard, they were falling over each other.

"I think he needs to twirl a little faster," the tall guy said.

"Like this?" Mike yanked my arm, spinning me so fast that I fell over.

"Yeah," the tall guy said, laughing so hard he could barely get the words out. "Now do the thing where you pick him up over your head and throw him back down to see if he lands on his feet."

Mike started to walk toward me with a wicked smile on his face. I knew there were only two choices: dance or run. I looked for an opening in the circle, then burst through it.

I was a good runner, light and quick, and they were

laughing too hard to chase me. But I kept on running anyway, until a shadow started to grow in the back of my mind. It felt like something heavy pressing down on me, and as I slowed down, my chest burning, gasping for breath, I knew what the shadow was. Even if I did get home alive this time, sooner or later I was going to have to meet up with Jonah. If it wasn't tonight, it would be tomorrow, and if it wasn't tomorrow, it would be next week.

CHAPTER 17

There was a bad storm that night. It was still dark when the thunder woke me up to a river of rain streaming down my window. I tried to switch on the light, but the power had gone out. I was too embarrassed to go to my mother's room and too frightened to stay in mine. So I crept downstairs, feeling my way along the banister with occasional flashes of lightning to guide me.

When I opened the front door to see if the other houses on the street had lost power, the wind nearly ripped the storm door from my hand. All the houses were dark, and there had been so much rain that the streets were flooded. A bolt of lightning lit up the whole yard and gave the lions in front of our house an eerie glow. I slammed the door shut, then went over and curled up on the sofa, pulling the afghan over my head. I don't know exactly when I fell asleep, but when I woke up the next morning, it was still dark and it was still raining.

My mom gave me a ride to school that day so I

wouldn't get wet walking or waiting for the bus. "I've got a big caseload today, so I'll probably be late," she said as she swung our red Volvo into a parking space in front of the school. "Would you call me to let me know you got home okay?"

"Sure."

I could feel her studying me. "Are you feeling all right, Tucker? It's not like you to spend the night on the sofa."

"I'm fine. It was just the storm. I couldn't sleep."

She paused a minute. "Is your science fair project going well?"

"I'm not exactly getting the results I expected."

"That's how the greatest discoveries are made. If we always got what we expected, we'd never learn anything new." She smiled and put her hand on my arm. "Take it easy, okay?"

My mom peered through the windshield, then turned on the wipers so she could see better.

"Tucker . . . isn't that your friend Angelo over there?"

I squinted through the wipers at a figure hunched over near the curb.

"Looks like him."

"I wonder what in the world he's doing."

"I don't know, but I'll find out."

I got out of the car, tucked my books and both lunches inside my rain jacket and pulled the hood up over my head. Then I walked over to Pig as my mom pulled away. He had his back to me and was drenched with rain.

At first I was afraid that Jonah might have gotten to

him. Then I saw that he wasn't bent over in pain. He was crouching down to pick worms out of the gutter.

"Are you crazy?" I said. "What are you doing that for?"

"It's a surprise, for Beth Ellen," he said, rescuing a wriggly one from the water that was flowing into the sewer and dropping it into the open can he held in his other hand.

A bunch of kids were getting off the bus and running into the school. As I watched them go by, pointing at us, I realized with a sickening feeling that it was the north side bus and that the last person off the bus was going to be Jonah.

"Get up," I said.

"What? Why?"

"Just get up, I'll explain later."

But it was too late. Jonah was getting off the bus and walking toward us.

"Well, if it isn't the pig and the pygmy. What's this," he said, staring down into Pig's can of worms, "your lunch? Man, you'll eat anything."

"I'm collecting them for someone," Pig said.

"Here's a good one for you," Jonah said. He stopped over, picked up a worm and held it in front of Pig's face. Then he flung it into the street just as a big truck went rumbling by, crushing it.

"Cut it out, Jonah," Pig said angrily.

"Angelo Pighetti, defender of the worms," Jonah said. "Bet you didn't know they could fly." He picked up another worm and pitched it hard against the brick wall.

"I said, cut it out," Pig yelled, wiping away the water that was streaming down his face as he knelt by the curb.

Jonah's eyes fixed on a big, fat earthworm that was slithering across the sidewalk. He walked toward it slowly, deliberately. Then he rested his heel on the sidewalk with his foot poised and ready to come down on the worm.

"Did you hear that?" Jonah said. "I think he's calling you. 'Help me, Pig, help me.'"

Jonah started to lower his foot an inch at a time. Pig looked like he was frozen to the spot, watching the worm crawl slowly across the sidewalk under Jonah's descending foot. Jonah was just about to squash it when I saw Pig's whole body come flying though the air. He landed flat out on the sidewalk and stuck his hand between the worm and Jonah's boot. Jonah pressed down hard on his knuckles, pushing them against the sidewalk, then twisting his foot as though he were crushing a cigarette butt into the ground.

"You stupid scum," Jonah said, spitting the words at Pig as he lay on the sidewalk.

Then Jonah turned and stared at me with a look so full of cruelty that I hope I never have to see it in anyone's eyes again.

"This is from the hyenas," he said. He pulled his fist back and took a swing at me, but I jumped out of the way and he just grazed me. He took another shot at my stomach, but I spun around so he missed again.

"Stand still, you stupid idiot," he shouted. He stuck his jaw out and took another swing, aiming at my face, but I jerked my head back and he lost his balance and fell down. Jonah got up on his hands and knees. He was dirty and dripping wet. "So you think you know something about fighting, Harrison?" He stood up, facing me. "Take a look at that."

I turned to see what he was pointing at, and he caught me with his other fist square in the gut, knocking me off my feet. He looked down at me with contempt. "You're not even worth beating up," he said, and he shoved me with his foot. Then he walked toward the school, leaving Pig and me alone in the rain.

Pig sat on the curb, cradling his hand, which was dripping with mud and blood. I was shaking with fear and anger.

"Why do you keep getting into this stuff?" I snarled. "I don't know why I thought I could ever help you, Pig."

"*You*—help *me*?" he said. His face was streaming with dirty tears. "Just forget the whole thing if that's what you think this is all about, Tucker. Because I don't need the kind of help you give people. I was happy being who I was, and I could be happy again if you'd just quit treating me like your dumb guinea pig and leave me alone."

"I—I didn't mean . . . ," I stammered, trying to back out of the hole I had just dug for myself.

"I did," Pig said. "I don't want to be fixed, Tucker. And I sure don't want to stand in the way of your scientific career. Either find yourself another experiment or find yourself another fat boy."

He struggled to his feet, still clutching his sore hand. I

held out his lunch bag as a peace offering, but he took it out of my hand, threw it at my feet and walked away.

"Wait," I called after him. "Maybe I can help you." But there was no one left to hear me, just the rain and the empty street.

CHAPTER 18

ig didn't show up for lunch. When I couldn't find him after school either, I called the Pighettis' restaurant and asked if I could stop by and see him, but they told me he'd come home sick and gone to bed.

I went to the kitchen to make myself a snack and found a note on the counter from my mom, telling me my dad had arranged a layover and wanted to see me at seven. If I stayed home alone all afternoon, I knew all I would do was worry about the mess I had made of everything. So instead I decided to ride my bike to the Hunan Palace and return Mr. Wong's *Handbook of Chinese Horoscopes*. It was four when I got there, too early for customers to be arriving for dinner. The rain had stopped, but the streets were slick and the sky was still dark and gloomy. For the first time all day, I relaxed as I stepped into the darkness and peace of the restaurant. The wind chimes over the door tinkled as I brushed past them, and I could hear voices in the kitchen laughing and talking in Chinese, which always seemed to me like a song. The busboys, who usually went back and forth to and from the kitchen as though someone had switched them to fast forward, seemed to be in no particular hurry as they folded napkins, set out silverware and packed fortune cookies into little waxed-paper bags.

Behind the counter Mr. Wong sat on a stool, polishing the carvings he kept on a shelf by the cash register. They were little brown ovals, not much bigger than walnuts, and were carved in the shapes of all sorts of animals, dragons and temples, old Chinese men with long droopy mustaches and fat, smiling gods. He had laid them out in a row in front of him and was bent over them, wiping them one at a time with such careful attention that he didn't even look up when I walked in.

"Isn't he handsome?" Mr. Wong said. He was polishing a carving of a smiling, fat man, holding a fish the size of a large dog in his lap. "His name is Ebitsu, the Japanese god of cooks and restaurants. He has great wisdom and compassion, but he also has one great fault. He loves to eat fish."

"I like him," I said. "He reminds me of a friend of mine."

Mr. Wong smiled as he took Ebitsu and placed him back on the shelf.

"He is one of my favorites too. What to one man is a great vice, to another is a great virtue. Will you be joining us for dinner tonight, Tucker?"

"No. I came to return your book," I said, setting it on the counter.

"Did you find what you needed in it?"

"It was interesting. But it didn't solve my problem."

"Perhaps you would like to talk." He motioned for me to sit down on the stool next to him and handed me a cloth and a carving of two curled-up sleeping rabbits to polish.

"I'm working on a project at school and it's not turning out very well," I said.

"A problem of work," said Mr. Wong. "I thought it might be a problem of family."

"Well, really, it's kind of both," I said. "My father wants me to enroll in the State Math and Science Academy next year, and the only chance I have to be accepted is by winning a ribbon at the science fair."

"Your father is a very accomplished man. I can see why you respect his advice," Mr. Wong said, picking up a carving of a dark rat and a light rat curled up together.

"But I'm not even sure I want to go to the Math and Science Academy."

"Yes, I see," said Mr. Wong, sighing as he polished the carving. "You must also listen to your heart."

"And even if I was sure I wanted to go, I couldn't win a ribbon at the science fair, at least not with the project I'm working on now. The more I work on it, the worse it gets."

Mr. Wong nodded slowly.

"It seems that you have reached a crisis," he said.

He got up and went to a drawer, took out a brush and a box of watercolors, then came back and laid my hand flat on the counter.

"The Chinese word for crisis is written with two characters," he said.

He made several sharp black brush strokes on the back of my hand.

"The first is the symbol for danger," he said. Mr. Wong rubbed his brush back in the paint, then made a number of squiggly lines with something that looked like a roof over the top of them. "The second is the symbol for movement, change and opportunity. Remember that the seeds of both are present in every crisis you encounter."

I stared at the marks on my hand. "I think you made the sharp lines too small and the squiggly lines too big," I said. "I seem to be running into a whole lot more danger than opportunity."

Mr. Wong smiled as he wiped off his brush on a piece of paper and closed the paint box. "You will survive the danger and prosper, Tucker. You are a rat. Rats can always be counted on in a crisis. Coping with difficulties brings out their best qualities: cleverness and ambition."

He put the rest of the carvings back on the shelf, then came around the corner to walk me to the door. "Just beware of the rat's darker side, his negative qualities."

"What are they?" I asked.

Mr. Wong put a hand on my shoulder and smiled. "His cleverness and ambition."

CHAPTER 19

The phone was ringing when I walked in the house. I threw my books on the hall table and ran into the kitchen to answer it.

"Hi, Tucker," my mom said. "Is everything all right?"

"Uh-huh."

"I was beginning to get worried about you," she said. "I've been trying to reach you since four-thirty."

"I went to the Hunan Palace to return a book to Mr. Wong."

"How's the last report on your science fair project coming along? Do you think you'll be finished on time?" my mom asked.

"Absolutely," I said. "In fact, if things keep going like they have been, I might be finished even sooner than I think."

"Great. I want to hear all about it when I get home tonight. Did you get the note I left you? I stopped home

145

for lunch and your dad called. He's changing planes here and thought he'd have time to see you at around seven."

"I'll be waiting."

"The ever-reliable Tucker Harrison," my mom said. "I won't rush home. Maybe I'll order a sandwich from the deli and stay at the office this evening. I can use the extra time to get some paperwork done."

"I'd better go then," I said. "I have to do some homework before he comes."

"Right," she said. "Have a good time. I'll see you around nine o'clock."

I went upstairs, then remembered I hadn't checked the answering machine in my mother's study.

"You have one message," the voice said when I pressed the Play button. Then it beeped and played it.

"Tucker, this is Dad. Sorry to have to let you down like this—"

I pressed my finger down hard on the Pause button and held my hand there trying to decide whether to choose Repeat or Erase. It seemed like a waste of time to listen to the rest of the message when I knew exactly what he was going to say. My fingers hovered for a while over the buttons before I decided to play the whole thing.

"Tucker, this is Dad. Sorry to have to let you down like this, but I won't be able to see you tonight after all. Something's come up and I have to take an earlier plane back to Boston. I'll see you soon, though . . . at the science fair."

The machine beeped and the phony voice came back again.

"That was your last message," it said.

I slapped at the button again and played the message over and over, as though there were some secret hidden in it and if I just listened to it long enough I might figure out what it was.

"Tucker, this is Dad. Tucker, this is Dad. . . . back to Boston. Something's come up . . . Sorry to have to let you down. Sorry to have to let you down."

"No, you're not sorry," I shouted, stabbing at the last button on the phone.

"Erasing message," the phone answered obediently. "That was your last message."

I slumped into the chair behind my mother's desk and spun it around to look out the window of her study. Most of the trees were bare now, and the street was deserted. I tried to make my mind stay just like that, quiet and empty, but pictures kept flashing through my mind: my father on the plane flying back to Boston; my mom in her office eating dinner alone; Beth Ellen saying I'd better not hurt Angelo; that horrible look in Jonah's eyes.

I thought about going to the Pighettis', standing in the darkness, outside the warmth and light and music of the restaurant, trying to decide whether or not to go in. Then I thought about Ms. Bodine saying, "I'm going out on a limb for you, Tucker."

I looked around me at the rows of books that lined the walls of my mother's study. There was something reassuring about just being there behind the big walnut desk, with all those shelves that had so much knowledge neatly

147

stacked on them. I leaned back in the chair and closed my eyes to let the feeling sink in.

I knew I couldn't win the science fair. The first two parts of my program had been dismal failures, and we hadn't even begun the exercise program. But for some reason, I didn't feel bad about that now. What I did feel bad about was losing Pig as a friend.

I opened my science project notebook and Ms. Bodine's warning stared up at me from the first page: "First, do no harm." What was I going to tell her? Pig was four pounds fatter than when he started my diet, and if I didn't find some way to turn off his virtual imagination, there was no telling how much fatter he would get.

The one thing I knew for certain was that I had to try to undo some of the damage I'd done. Even if my science fair project was all washed up, even if Pig never wanted to be my friend again, I owed him that much at least.

I went to the shelves and pulled down an armload of books at random and settled back into the welcome firmness of my mother's brown leather chair. All I had to do was think like a professional, I told myself. What would it be like if I were really a psychiatrist?

"Ms. Dingleberg," I imagined myself barking into the intercom. "Send in my next patient.

"Ah, yes. Mr. Pig," I would say, rising to pull out a chair for him. "Come in. Come in. How was your week? Good . . . good . . . good. Any new symptoms? Too bad. Yes, well, I believe I have the answer to your problems right here."

I selected a book from the top of the stack. "*The Inter-*

pretation of Dreams, by Sigmund Freud," I mumbled to myself. "No, that will take too long, and besides, I don't have a couch. What's this one? Carl Rogers *On Becoming a Person.* I didn't know you needed an instruction book. No wonder I'm having so many problems. I thought it happened automatically.

"How about this," I said, picking up a fat volume with a blue cover and gold embossed letters. "*Abnormal Psychology, Dictionary of Current Treatment and Practice.* That sounds about right, doesn't it?" I asked, dropping it on the desk with a thud.

"Let us begin at the beginning," I said to the imaginary Mr. Pig, turning to the A section. "A is for addiction, adolescence . . . I didn't know that was a disease, did you? . . . alcoholism . . . aversion therapy. . . . Wait a minute. That's it.

" 'Aversion therapy: a treatment in which an unpleasant stimulus is repeatedly coupled with an undesired behavior in order to eliminate the behavior. In alcoholism, for example, vomit-inducing drugs have been injected at the same time as alcohol is taken to produce associations of nausea . . .' "

My mind was racing. If I could make fattening food seem yucky to Pig, he wouldn't want to eat it and the problem would be solved. I couldn't give him drugs that made him throw up, of course, but maybe there was another way. I hurried down to the kitchen, turned on the oven and started pulling things out of the cabinet. Bowl, brownie mix, measuring cup . . .

I tore open the box, poured in the brownie mix and oil,

grabbed some eggs out of the refrigerator, then scanned the shelves for something really bad.

"Yes! Louisiana hot sauce," I said out loud, grabbing the bottle and shaking half of it into the batter.

Then I opened the cabinet, grabbed the can of chili powder and the can of red pepper and poured those in too. With wicked enthusiasm, I stirred red swirls into the thick, brown batter. Then I stopped. A horrible thought flashed through my mind. What would it be like when Pig actually ate this stuff? Well, I thought as I wiped up the batter that had slopped over the side of the bowl, maybe he would be angry for a while. But he was already pretty angry, and when he realized that I'd fixed whatever it was I'd done that had made him eat even more, maybe he'd get over it. Sometimes you have to do things people don't like in order to help them.

I put in a few more shakes of chili powder and added some garlic for good measure. Then I scraped the whole bowl into a pan. Now if I could just get Pig to eat it, I thought. Everything in my life was riding on one batch of brownies.

CHAPTER 20

I waited outside Pig's math class the next day with the box of brownies under my arm, feeling like someone who was about to deliver a package with a bomb in it.

The class was late getting out. Through the window of the closed door, I could see Mr. Humphrey pointing at the blackboard with one hand, then pushing his glasses back up his nose with the other hand. He did this over and over in a kind of dance: point, push, point, push. I couldn't hear what he was saying, but I could see his mouth moving, and I kept looking at his lips, hoping to read the words "Class dismissed." In between I stole quick glances down the hallway, as though someone were about to arrest me for possession of dangerous brownies.

Finally Mr. Humphrey put the chalk down. At the same instant, the door burst open and a crowd of kids raced out like prisoners seizing their last chance to escape. They seemed afraid that the doors of math class would be closed and locked for good and they would have to spend the rest of their lives in there, trying to memorize the formula for the area of a circle.

Pig ambled out last, after everyone else had disappeared down the hall. He looked at me with mild surprise.

"What are you doing here?"

"I'm sorry about the way I treated you yesterday. I was just discouraged. I thought . . . I don't know . . . that it would be easier than this."

Pig half smiled at me. "Yeah . . . well, things aren't always easy."

I looked down at his bandaged fingers. "How's your hand?" I asked.

"Okay."

I wanted to say something to make him feel better, but I couldn't think of anything. So I decided to tell him about my new idea. "I've got good news, Pig. I know how to help you lose weight now."

Pig looked disgusted. "Give it up, Tucker. The experiment is over."

"But I really think this can work."

Pig stopped walking and turned to face me.

"Forget it. Just write up all your research on fat kids and go present that at the science fair. You probably won't take home any ribbons, but maybe they'll give you an honorable mention. Then you can go back to living your life and I can go back to mine."

He started to walk away from me, but I caught him by the arm.

"It's not for the science fair," I said. "This is for you . . . to make up for the weight I made you gain and the way I messed up your mind."

I handed him the box. "What would you say if I told you I had something in here that was guaranteed to make you want to stop eating junk food?"

He stared at the box.

"Open it," I said. "Go ahead. What have you got to lose?"

I folded my arms and waited. Finally Pig pried off the top.

"I think you gave me the wrong box," Pig said, peering over the lid. "These are brownies."

"Ahhh, but they're no ordinary brownies. All you have to do is eat one of those brownies and you won't want another taste of chocolate for a long, long time."

Pig wrinkled his forehead. "Right. Magic brownies."

"If you don't believe me, try it. Eat one brownie. I promise that's the last thing I'll ask you to do. If it works, you lose weight, and if it doesn't I won't bother you again."

Pig looked at the brownies. "You promise you won't bug me about this again if I eat one?"

I nodded.

"Well," he said, "they do look good." He reached in and pulled one out. The whole world seemed to slow down as he raised the moist, chocolaty brownie, with its explosive contents, closer to his lips. His mouth opened. Then he stopped. He sniffed the brownie pensively.

"These are different," he said. He turned the brownie around in his hand, then sniffed again. "They smell like chocolate . . . but something else, too. Something I can't quite put my finger on."

For an instant I thought it was all over. He put his nose very close to the brownie and took a deep breath.

"Whatever it is, it's something I really like. Thanks, Tucker." Pig opened his mouth again and was about to take a bite. Then suddenly a hand grabbed his wrist and jerked it, knocking the brownie onto the floor.

"What have we here?" Jonah asked, taking the box of brownies out of Pig's other hand. "Did you make these just for me?"

Pig scowled at him.

"Tucker made them. For *me.*"

"Ohhhh, how sweet," Jonah said. "A present for the little piglet. You don't mind if my friends and I have a few, do you, swine?"

"I wouldn't eat those if I were you," I said.

"But you're not me, are you, Shrinky Dink?"

Jonah took a brownie out of the box. I lunged at him, trying to get it away before he could eat it, but one of his friends grabbed me from behind and pinned my arms behind my back.

"You'd better be careful," Jonah said. "You could get hurt acting like that."

He stood directly in front of me, threw his shoulders back and smiled a thin-lipped smile. Then he opened his mouth wide. He seemed to become all teeth and tongue. He popped the whole brownie into his mouth and swallowed it in one big gulp. Slowly a look of pain and terror

154

spread over his face. He let out a huge yelp like a dog run over by a truck and put both hands on his throat.

"Waaaaaa," he gasped, pointing at his limp tongue with his finger.

His friends looked stupidly at him, unable to understand what he was trying to say.

"Waaaaaaaa," he screamed.

His eyes darted around the hall and finally found what they were looking for. He ran full speed for the water fountain and put his whole face in, letting the water rush over his open mouth and out again, trying to put out the fire on his tongue. Sputtering and gasping for breath, he turned back toward us and charged directly at me, his eyes burning with rage.

Jonah reached out and grabbed my shirt with one hand and swung at my face with the other. His friends let go of my arms and I slumped to the floor, but he picked me up and shoved me down the hall with a foot to my stomach. Dazed and out of breath, I lifted my head and watched as he came toward me again.

Then everything seemed to stop. I heard an angry roar and saw someone come up behind Jonah, lift him up by his jacket and slam him against the lockers.

It was Pig.

He spun Jonah around like a limp doll and pinned him against the lockers with his shoulder, the full force of his great weight pressing on Jonah's chest.

"Lemme go, Pig," Jonah gasped. "I can't breathe."

No one made a move to help Jonah. Everyone stood

still, waiting to see what Pig would do next. There was a long, anxious silence. Then Pig murmured something into Jonah's face.

"My name is Angelo Pighetti," he said.

Jonah just stared at him.

"Say it."

"What?"

"My name is Angelo Pighetti."

"My name is . . . Angelo Pighetti," Jonah wheezed at him.

"No, you dummy. Your name is Jonah. My name is Angelo Pighetti, and you're never going to call me Pig again. Say my name."

"Angelo Pighetti," Jonah mumbled.

"Louder."

"Angelo Pighetti."

Slowly Pig released the pressure and lowered Jonah back to the ground. Jonah sat leaning against the locker in a heap, rubbing his chest and breathing hard. Pig took a few steps backward, looked over his shoulder at me, then started to walk off in the other direction.

"Hey, wait," I called out to him, struggling to my feet and hurrying after him.

He turned toward me. "You made those brownies for me," he snarled.

"I just wanted to help you. It was the only thing left, the only thing I could think to do."

"I'm just like one of those lab rats to you. Something that doesn't feel pain, so you can go ahead and do whatever you want to it."

"Th-That's not true," I stammered. "Maybe it started out that way . . . at the beginning . . . before . . . when I wasn't your friend . . . but—"

"You don't know how to be anyone's friend," he interrupted. "You don't care who you hurt, or why, just as long as you get what you want."

Pig glanced at Jonah, who was still slumped against the locker.

"You're even worse than he is. At least he was honest about wanting to hurt me. But you're still pretending to be my friend."

He started to walk away, and I grabbed him by the arm.

"Pig, stop," I said.

He looked back at me, his eyes flashing with rage.

"My name is Angelo Pighetti," he said, jerking his arm away from my grasp.

Then he turned and walked slowly down the hall.

CHAPTER 21

I sat on the steps after school and watched as the last few kids got on my bus, laughing and pushing each other as they struggled to get to the best seats. The driver closed the door behind them to keep the cold air out and sat with the motor running awhile longer, looking for stragglers. Then, with a loud grinding sound, she put the bus in gear and pulled away from the curb. I thought I saw someone wave to me out of a side window and felt a sudden urge to get up and run after the bus, but just as quickly the urge left me. It wasn't that I had anywhere to go or anything to do. All I knew was that I didn't want to go home.

When the crowd of kids outside the school dwindled down to one or two, I was still sitting there. I heard footsteps coming up behind me and turned to see who it was, afraid that it might be Jonah. But it was Beth Ellen staring down at me.

"Why aren't you in Ms. Bodine's office with the rest of them?" she asked, folding her arms.

"What do you mean?"

"Angelo and Jonah got called in for fighting. I guess Ms. Bodine didn't know that the real problem was you."

"I know you're not going to believe me, Beth Ellen, but I really was trying to help Angelo."

Beth Ellen sat down on the step next to me, leaned back and propped herself up with her elbows. "You didn't want to help him, Tucker. You just wanted to win the science fair."

I rubbed some mud off the toe of my shoe. "That was what I thought I wanted . . . but not if it meant Angelo was going to get hurt."

Beth Ellen sat up and pulled her cape in closer to her body. "You did hurt him, Tucker."

"I know, and I was trying to put things back together again. Didn't you ever hurt someone you like and then you didn't know how to fix it?" She twisted one of her earrings and shrugged.

A gust of wind came up, and I buried my face in my sleeve to keep warm. "It wasn't just the science fair, Beth Ellen. I wanted to help Angelo because he's my friend."

I could feel her eyes studying my face.

"The sad part is I honestly believe you're telling the truth." She stood up and hoisted her backpack onto her shoulder. "I've got to get home and feed my worms. Maybe you should go home too."

"I'll get around to it eventually," I said.

Beth Ellen started to walk down the steps; then she turned back. "You know the one thing Angelo knows that you don't? It's a come-as-you-are party, Tucker."

"What is?"

"Life . . . friendship . . . everything."

Since I had no place to go after Beth Ellen left, it was easy to figure out how to get there. It was a cold, cloudy November day. The wind stung my cheeks, so I kept my head down, watched my feet, and kept walking the rest of the afternoon. I didn't even notice where I was until I stopped at a corner, looked up and saw Wechsler Park across the street. I shoved my hands deep into my pockets to keep them warm and walked through the big iron gate and up the path that led to the veterans' memorial at the top of the hill.

It was dusk and the lights on either side of the walk were starting to come on, with a dull glow that made the memorial barely visible against the gray sky. From down the hill I could see the statues of the four branches of service: a sailor looking out to sea with his hands cupped over his eyes, a marine planting a flag on a beach, a soldier raising his rifle in the air, and a pilot with his hand held over his heart. I climbed up to the top of the hill, then boosted myself up on the monument and sat down between them, staring at the dull sky.

The lights were beginning to come on in the buildings below me. Everything seemed so distant and small from up on the hill. It was the first time all day I had felt relaxed and at peace. I hugged my knees to my chest and let the time slip away without worrying about where I had to go or what I had to do.

I was so wrapped up in my problems that it never occurred to me I might be creating new ones by staying out so late, until I turned down my street and saw the police car parked in front of my house. I stopped dead when I saw it, and thought about going back. But there didn't seem to be a place to go back to anymore. Like it or not, I had to go forward.

Mrs. Hrabik threw open the door when I rang the bell.

"Mrs. boy!" she said, throwing her arms around me in a bear hug that lifted me off the floor.

She slapped both hands on her cheeks and started crying and muttering nonstop, with now and then a word slipped in that I could understand.

"I crazy . . . Mrs. boy gone . . . everybody look . . . everybody cry."

She went running into the living room and came back, pulling my mother by the arm.

"See? Mrs. boy home."

My mother's face was limp with shock and relief. "Tucker. Where *have* you been?" she demanded, pressing a damp cheek against mine. "I've been worried sick about you. Mrs. Hrabik paged me when you didn't come home for supper. We looked everywhere, called everyone we knew. I was so worried I even notified the police."

The policeman appeared in the hallway, stuffing his pen in his coat pocket.

"I'm sorry, Officer. I owe you an apology. And my son

does too," she said, glaring at me. It looked like the shocked and relieved part was over and the angry part was about to begin.

"Not at all, Mrs. Harrison," he said, folding up his evidence book. "I'm just glad this case had a happy ending. Not all of them do."

He picked up his hat from the hall table and walked to the door; then he turned back to me. "You had these ladies very upset, son. I think they're the ones who deserve an apology. Good night, Mrs. Harrison. Thank you for the coffee, ma'am," he said, tipping his hat in Mrs. Hrabik's direction.

After he closed the door, Mrs. Hrabik went to get her things out of the closet. My mother went over and gave her a big hug. "Thank you, Mrs. Hrabik. I don't know what I would have done without you. Why don't you stay and share that wonderful meal you made with us?"

"No good stomach," Mrs. Hrabik said, wrinkling her face and clutching her middle.

"You'd better go home and rest then," I blurted out.

My mother flashed me another one of her looks.

"No, please, go upstairs and lie down in my bedroom. I'll just go in the kitchen and make you a nice hot cup of tea," she said.

"Such good woman," Mrs. Hrabik said, putting her hand on my mother's cheek. Then she pulled on her knit cap and came over and patted me on the cheek.

"Mommy love you," she said. "I love you. Be good boy. I go home. Sleep. Wake up. All better now."

It was funny how Mrs. Hrabik was able to say everything she needed to using only fifty or so English words. It made you wonder why the dictionary was so fat.

My mother drove Mrs. Hrabik home, and I went in the kitchen and found two places already set. I lifted the lid of the large black pot that was sitting on the cooktop and poked around at the boiled beef and cabbage inside with a wooden spoon. It was cold, and there was a thin film forming on the top that looked like an oil slick. It must have been sitting there for several hours. I turned on the gas, hoping to improve it by heating it, then set out the salad Mrs. Hrabik had left in the refrigerator and some biscuits she'd kept warm for us in the oven. When my mom came back, I was slumped on one of the stools, like a condemned man with nothing to look forward to but his last meal.

"Okay," she said, pulling up the stool across from me, "I'm listening."

"I guess that means I'm talking," I said.

She gave a little crooked smile and nodded.

"You want to know why I came home so late."

"That would be a good place to start," she said.

"I was upset. I needed to think, so I went for a walk over near Wechsler Park. I didn't want to worry you. I just lost track of the time."

My mom sat quietly for a while.

"Does your being upset have anything to do with Angelo?"

"Did he tell you that?"

"When you didn't come home, I called the Pighettis.

Angelo said you had gotten into some sort of fight with a group of boys at school."

I looked down at my hands.

"Angelo's mad at me too," I said.

"Oh?"

"About my science fair project. Actually about *being* my science fair project."

My mother looked sideways at me.

"I don't think I understand," she said.

"That's because it was supposed to be a secret. But I might as well tell you, since it's all going down the drain anyway." I took a deep breath and plunged in. "I didn't think I could win the science fair with my weight loss project unless I came up with some sort of really good gimmick. And the gimmick I came up with was putting Angelo on a diet. The only problem was Angelo didn't want to lose weight. He only went along with it to help me out."

I hesitated a minute. It felt so good to finally tell someone the truth that I had a sudden urge to blurt out all of it.

My mother sat for a moment with both hands covering her face. When she finally spoke it sounded like the sentence was a puzzle that wouldn't quite fit together.

"You . . . made your friend your . . . science fair project."

"I thought it would be good for both of us. I'd win the science fair and he'd lose weight. I just didn't know how hard it was to fix people the way you do."

"Fix people? But that isn't what I do at all," she said.

She threw up her hands and stared at the ceiling as if she were waiting for something to fall. Then she dropped them into her lap.

"I really messed up, didn't I?"

"No, Tucker," she said, reaching out to put her hand over mine. "You just didn't understand. If I had been paying more attention when you first got started on this project . . ." She leaned back in her chair and sighed.

"Let me explain something, Tucker. A therapist isn't someone with a cookie cutter who sits in her office stamping out people who look exactly alike, trimming a little here or adding a little there until they fit someone else's idea of what's normal."

She stopped and thought a moment. "How can I say this?" She brushed the hair out of my eyes. "Do you know why I love you?"

"Because I'm smart. And because I think for myself. And because I'm your kid so you have to."

"Uh-uh," she said, shaking her head. "I love you because you're smart, and sometimes foolish; you're funny and wise, but also sad and angry and sometimes crazy—because you're good at Ping-Pong, bad at checkers, a whiz at school but you never study. Because sometimes you talk too little and sometimes you talk too much—because you remember my birthday but you always forget to make your bed. I love you because you're all of those things and a whole lot more, good and bad, beautiful and ugly, difficult, delightful, the whole package, and no one in the whole world knows how to be Tucker Harrison except you."

"So—what's this got to do with me trying to help Angelo lose weight so he can be happy?"

"Don't you see? It wasn't wrong for you to want Angelo to be happy, Tucker. What was wrong was not letting Angelo decide for himself what that means."

My mother waited for me to look up again, then caught my eye.

"Do you understand, Tucker?"

"I'm beginning to," I said in a low voice. "But I think it's too late to do anything about it."

"It's never too late." She smiled at me. "People are always learning. Growing up isn't like taking a test on fractions. You can't flunk. If you don't get it the first time, you just go back in there and try again."

"That's not how the science fair works, though. And I won't get into the State Math and Science Academy if I blow this."

She looked carefully at me.

"Is that what you want . . . to go to the academy?"

"It's what Dad wants, and Ms. Bodine thinks it would be good for me. I thought you wanted it too."

"That's not the point. What matters is what you want."

She put her hand on my cheek. "Oh, Tucker," she said, "maybe you're not the only one who has to redo this lesson."

"Everyone is counting on me to win this. I don't know what to do."

My mom stood up and pushed her chair back to the counter.

"It seems to me you have some thinking to do."

166

She put her arm around my shoulder.

"I know you'll make a good decision, and whatever you choose, I'll back you up," she said. "Now how about a little late supper?"

"No thanks," I said, suddenly feeling completely exhausted. "I'm too tired to eat. I think I'll just go right to bed."

I went upstairs, switched off the light, crawled into bed and stared at the ceiling for a while.

My mom was right. No one knew how to be Tucker Harrison except me. That's why it seemed like such a lonely job.

CHAPTER 22

I set my alarm for five-thirty the next morning so I could write a note apologizing to Angelo. After writing and tearing up six or seven long explanations, I finally just scribbled "Sorry I was a jerk" on a piece of paper and folded it up. That seemed to sum things up pretty well. I knew he wouldn't change his mind about me, no matter what I said.

When my mom woke up, I was already downstairs having breakfast. She walked into the kitchen in her robe, yawning, and poured herself a glass of juice. I was drizzling syrup over my waffles, trying to get a little dot in each square, but it kept spilling out over the sides.

"You're up awfully early," she said, setting her glass on the counter and sitting down next to me. "How are things looking after a good night's rest?"

"Gloomy," I mumbled to my plate.

She reached over with her fork, stabbed a bite I had just cut off for myself and popped it in her mouth.

"Is there some kind of worldwide waffle shortage going on, or did I just get the last one in the box?" I snapped.

"Wait a minute," she said, lifting my chin with one finger. "Let me see those dark circles under your eyes. Looks like you didn't get much sleep last night. You okay?"

"If I say no will you call Ms. Bodine and tell her I'm too sick to go to school?"

She put her hand on my forehead to see if it was hot. "Not a chance."

"That's what I was afraid of," I said.

My mom took a sip of orange juice, studying me carefully. "You know the hardest thing I ever had to learn?"

"What?" I asked, not really wanting to hear, because I was afraid I was about to find out for myself.

"That sometimes you have to keep putting one foot in front of the other even when you don't know where to go or what to do."

She went over to the freezer, took out the box of waffles and looked inside.

"Empty," she said, raising one eyebrow at me. "Maybe there is a waffle shortage. I hope it hasn't affected the toast supply yet."

I left the house early so I could get to school to talk to Ms. Bodine before class started and still have time to stop at the Pighettis' on the way. The kitchen door was open, so I slipped in quietly, laid the note for Angelo on the counter, and turned to leave. Then I heard opera music coming from the restaurant. When I pushed open the door a crack, I saw Mr. Pighetti sitting at a table in the shadows. It was too dark to tell for sure, but I thought I saw tears covering his face.

"Is everything all right?" I asked, stepping inside.

"La Bohème," he said, pointing at the speaker. "I can't play it when the restaurant's open because it always makes me cry."

"It must be really sad."

"Very." He nodded. "It's about four poor starving friends in Paris: an artist, a poet, a philosopher and a musician. They have so little money they have to burn their books and furniture to keep warm. The poet, Rodolfo, falls in love with Mimi, a beautiful young girl who is very sick. But he is so sad that he can't give her good food and a warm, clean place to live that he leaves her rather than watch her die."

We sat quietly together while the orchestra played; then a man began singing in a rich, deep voice and Mr. Pighetti began crying again.

"What happened?" I said. "Is Mimi dead?"

"Not yet," Mr. Pighetti sobbed. "It's the philosopher, Colline. He's singing good-bye."

"To Mimi?"

"No, to his coat."

I raised my eyebrows. "He's singing to his coat?"

Mr. Pighetti wiped his tears away with a napkin and nodded. "He's taking it to the pawnshop to get money. He calls the coat 'fedele amico,' faithful friend. And he says thank you to it. 'Le mie grazie ricevi.'

170

"It's a great sacrifice. Colline lives in that coat. It protects him and keeps him warm. It has pockets for his papers and books of philosophy, all of the things that matter to him. He even sleeps in it. Now he's going to sell it to buy medicine for Mimi, because he loves his friend, Rodolfo, and Rodolfo loves Mimi. Friends are what really count in life, right, *amico mio*? It's easy to find a good coat, but not so easy to find a good friend." He put his hand on my shoulder.

"What about Mimi? Does Rodolfo ever see her again?"

Mr. Pighetti nodded slowly. "Just before she dies, Rodolfo tells her the truth, and she forgives him. Because she knows that even if what he did was wrong, he did it out of love for her."

"I think I'd be too angry to forgive him."

"Me too," Mr. Pighetti said sadly. "Me too."

The school was empty and quiet when I got there. There were a few teachers in the office, clustered around the copy machine and the mailboxes, but they acted as though I weren't there. I just sat in the chair trying not to think because every time I did, I imagined the worst, which really wasn't necessary because sooner or later the worst was going to find me.

Finally Ms. Bodine appeared in the doorway, wearing a black suit and, around her neck, a bloodred scarf, the same color as her glasses.

"Come in, Tucker. I'm glad you stopped by," she said, closing the door behind me. "I was going to call you down this afternoon to make sure you have everything ready for the science fair. Is that what you wanted to talk to me about?"

I started to speak, but it felt like my mouth was full of cotton and the words couldn't get out.

"What?" Ms. Bodine said, leaning closer to hear my muffled voice.

I cleared my throat and tried to speak more loudly. "I want to withdraw my project from the science fair."

This time the words exploded out of my mouth. We both fell back in our chairs, stunned.

"Withdraw?" she whispered.

My head nodded up and down like it was on a spring and I had a sudden urge to grab hold of it with both hands to try and make it stop.

"The science fair," she muttered.

A terrible silence settled over the room. Ms. Bodine looked out the window at the bare trees and didn't speak. My mind, which I had kept on a leash until now, started to lurch completely out of control. I imagined her jumping up out of her seat and lunging for my throat or taking things off the shelves and throwing them at me. Maybe she would faint and crumple up like a rag doll in her chair, or perhaps leap out the window to her death. Fortunately her office was on the first floor.

"Would you mind telling me why?" she asked finally.

I stared at the backs of my hands as though they had the answer written on them.

"I'm going to lose anyway," I said. "My project is a failure. I don't know any more about how to help fat kids now than I did when I started. As a matter of fact, I think I know less."

The chair squeaked as I squirmed in it. Her pencil tapped out a nervous rhythm on the desk. "Tucker, is there any connection between your wanting to withdraw and the fight Angelo and Jonah had?"

"Didn't they tell you why they were fighting?"

"No . . . not the details."

"It was my fault," I said. "When I tried to get Angelo to lose weight the usual way and it didn't work, I got a little carried away."

Ms. Bodine had that "here we go again" look on her face.

"I tried a bunch of different things. But the one that caused the fight was the chili-powder brownies. I thought they'd work like aversion therapy and make Angelo hate junk food. But then Jonah ate one by accident. And . . . I guess you can figure out the rest."

She set her pencil down and folded her hands, and sat quietly a long time.

"I think it's a good idea for you to withdraw, Tucker," she said.

I waited, expecting her to say more, but she sat perfectly still, staring at me. Maybe she wasn't going to throw books after all. Maybe she felt sorry for me and was going to let me off the hook.

"Just like that?" I asked, not knowing whether to be relieved or terrified. "I don't have to go to the science fair tomorrow?"

"That," said Ms. Bodine, "is not what I said. You can

withdraw from the science fair, but I still want you to write up your project. *And* you'll have to go there tomorrow and tell them what you've learned."

I thought I had imagined all the frightening possibilities, but this one hadn't occurred to me.

"But I haven't learned anything. Nothing I've done has worked."

"Then you've learned at least one thing—how to fail," she said. "Disproving your hypothesis is as valuable as proving it, Tucker. Science is mostly a process of finding out what won't work. And I suspect there are other things you've learned too. If you give it some thought, I'm sure you'll come up with a few."

"I don't understand," I said.

"You will. It will take a long time, but you've made a good beginning. The first step to knowledge is realizing that you don't understand. I don't remember who said that, but it's the truth."

Either I was still in bed dreaming or I had finally pushed Ms. Bodine over the edge. "You'd better go to your first class now. Your presentation is scheduled for ten o'clock on Saturday."

"But—"

"I'll see you there, Tucker."

I nodded my head weakly. Then I stood up and walked out of the door to my doom.

CHAPTER 23

"Here we are," Mom said, pulling into the driveway in front of the science building at Western City College. There was a banner over the door that read, WELCOME SCIENCE FAIR PARTICIPANTS. "Got everything you need?"

"I've got everything I could squeeze into this," I said, holding up the briefcase she had loaned me, full of records I'd kept and research I'd done. "Although I'm not sure why I brought it all."

I slid out of the car onto the curb, and my mom leaned out over the seat to say good-bye. Her smile looked unconvincing, like one you would see on a nurse trying to cheer up a fatally ill patient.

"You never know what you're going to need," she said. "Besides, it will give you something to hold on to."

"Kind of like a life preserver that doesn't float," I muttered.

Her face relaxed into a real smile and she shook her head.

175

"Your dad's coming directly from the airport. Hope his plane wasn't late. You all right?"

I said yes, but I didn't mean it.

"Good luck, Tucker," she said. "We'll be out there pulling for you."

I pushed the car door closed and she gave me the thumbs-up sign through the window as she drove toward the parking area. Then I followed the crowd of people headed toward the main entrance.

The science fair participants were supposed to report to Room 111. There was a crowd of kids from all over the city, some of them talking and laughing, others sitting off by themselves, going over their notes or nervously watching the other people in the room, probably wishing like me that they could be somewhere else. I thought of asking one of them if they'd like to join me in an escape attempt, but they didn't look like the type who took risks.

I didn't see Beth Ellen. Apparently the entries in her division had presented earlier in the day. I almost wished that she were there, just so there would be at least one person I knew.

A man in a blue suit, wearing a tie that had beakers and chemical formulas written all over it, was checking people in at a table in the corner. He handed me a program and a list of contest rules and instructions. I sat down in one of the chairs that lined the walls of the room, stuck the rules in my briefcase and ran my finger down the program until I found my name. Tucker Harrison, Nutrition and Childhood Obesity, Washington Junior High. It was near the beginning. At least I wouldn't have to wait long to get it over with. The judges probably got cranky toward the end.

Just before the contest was to begin, the chairman of the science fair committee, a balding man with a fringe of white hair and thick glasses that made his eyes look zigzaggy, came in to welcome us all, give us some last-minute instructions and wish us good luck. While he was talking, the girl next to me leaned over and whispered in my ear.

She had long, perfectly straight hair, tied back behind her ears like Alice in Wonderland's, and she lisped a little from the braces on her teeth. "I hope he's interested in mold," she whispered, pointing at the box full of specimens she had on her lap.

"Don't worry," I assured her. "Almost everyone is."

After he left, they called the first contestant's name and he walked out with the man in the blue suit.

A boy with a buzz cut and a clip-on tie leaned over Alice in Wonderland to introduce himself to me. "I'm Dmitri. This is Nora," he said, nodding toward her. He held out his hand and shook mine with a little too much enthusiasm. "We're from Courtland Middle School."

"Washington Junior High," I said.

"She's mold. I'm acid rain. What about you?"

"I'm fat," I said.

Nora looked me over from head to toe and raised her eyebrows. "You don't look that bad to me," she said.

"Timothy Warren and Tucker Harrison," the man in the blue suit read off his clipboard.

"I've got to go," I said, picking up my briefcase. "That's me."

"Good luck," Dmitri said, slapping me on the shoulder.

"Don't worry. You look just fine," Nora added.

The blue suit took us across the hall and showed us the steps leading up to the stage. "Warren, you're next," the blue suit said. "When you hear the applause die down after this young woman finishes, walk out to the podium and give your presentation. Don't let the large audience throw you. The judges will be sitting stage left, so look at them when you speak and give it all you've got. Harrison, you do the same thing. Wait until the applause dies down. Warren will walk out the other side of the stage, and you can go in."

Almost on cue, the audience began to clap and the girl at the podium folded up her notebook and walked off. Timothy Warren straightened up his shoulders and walked out onto the stage. There was a round of polite applause to welcome him. He began his speech.

Then I thought about what I had to do and broke into a sweat. Something inside me said forget about withdrawing from the contest, try and piece together something from the notes I'd brought in my briefcase. Something. Anything.

Timothy Warren's speech was drawing to a close.

"In conclusion . . . ," he said.

I wanted to run out of the building and never stop. I wanted to be out on the street, my throat burning, my heart pounding, my head too blurred to think, running until I dropped.

"Harrison?" someone tapped me on the shoulder from behind and I jumped as though I'd been struck. It was the man in the blue suit. "Go ahead. He's finished."

I willed my feet to go forward, but they wouldn't move.

"This is it. You're on," he said, giving me a nudge forward.

The audience was silent as I walked slowly to the center of the stage, stepped up to the podium and looked out at the crowd waiting expectantly to hear what I had to say. I put down my mother's briefcase and looked over at the judges, then scanned the audience for a familiar face and found my mom, my dad and Ms. Bodine all sitting together in the third row. A sick feeling rose in the pit of my stomach. My father motioned with his hands for me to speak.

"I would like to withdraw my project from the competition," I blurted into the microphone, the words echoing through the hall.

A murmur rippled through the crowd. My father's eyes locked on mine. I felt like he would burn a hole in me with his stare.

"The subject of my experiment was a teenager suffering from obesity who suffered even more . . . that is, he became obeser . . . I mean, fatter . . . no, weightier." I cleared my throat. "He became a very weighty subject as the experiment progressed."

It seemed like every jaw in the room dropped open. I picked up my report and fumbled through it, looking for something that sounded scientific. "A fat-restricted diet was used to . . . well, I guess you could say it was used to restrict facts . . . or rather, fats . . . and, uh, control caloric consumption."

I dug in the briefcase, pulled out the transparencies I'd made and set one down on the overhead projector. "You can see by this . . . um . . . perfectly flat line that the results were disappointing . . . at best."

My hand was shaking as I traced the line with the laser pointer. I tried to steady it with my other hand, but the little red dot still danced all over the graph like a hyperactive pinball. I set the next graph down on the overhead and pointed at the gigantic line that had now begun its steady climb up the graph.

"The next diet tested the effect of high-fiber food on weight loss, using a specially designed oat bran and barley pasta. Unfortunately this experimental food proved to have certain . . . adhesive qualities, which caused . . . undesirable side effects . . . for example, lockjaw."

One of the judges leaned over and whispered something to another. At the back of the hall the door opened, letting in a stream of light, and a group of people came in and sat down. I wanted to believe it was the Pighettis, but I knew it wasn't.

"Luckily, the subject made a rapid recovery and was able to move his jaws well enough to gain more weight, even after I put him on a diet of imaginary food."

I put the next graph on the screen. It looked like a picture of Mount Everest. Several people laughed out loud before they caught themselves.

"Then I made a critical error in judgment. I felt guilty about what I had done to the subject. I mean, Angelo.

180

Angelo's my friend. At least he used to be. I wanted to get him back to where he started: right here." I pointed to the base of Mount Everest. "So I came up with an aversion-therapy plan. I was going to trick him into eating chili-powder brownies. Only another kid ate them by accident. Then he beat me up. That was on purpose."

I looked down at Ms. Bodine. She had her head on the back of the chair and was staring up at the ceiling. On either side of her, my parents were both gripping their armrests like they were in a plane that was about to crash. I hesitated, trying to find the words for what I wanted to say. Then I took a deep breath and plunged in.

"When I started this project, Ms. Bodine told me that science was a tool for helping people and I thought I knew what that meant. But it turns out helping people can be pretty complicated.

"I—I know all of this sounds pretty bad," I stammered. "But I was so convinced I knew what was right for Angelo that I talked myself into believing it was what he wanted too. I guess what I've learned from all this is that people have a right to decide for themselves who they are and what they want to be."

I glanced over at my father, looking for some reaction. His hand was shielding his eyes.

"But I had to pay a high price to learn it. I lost a good friend. That's all I have to say. Except, I'm sorry."

There was dead silence as I walked over and handed the report of my failed project to the judges. I started to leave, then I saw someone in the audience stand up. From the back of the auditorium Mr. Pighetti called out,

"Bravo! Bravo, amico mio!" One person, then two, then three joined him. Mr. Wong stood in the center of the audience, smiling and clapping. I saw Ms. Bodine stand up, applauding, and my mom, who seemed to be crying. Then my father rose to his feet, clapping slowly and deliberately, as I walked off the stage.

I left the auditorium and went outside so I could be alone for a while before I had to talk to my parents and Ms. Bodine. The science building was at the edge of the campus near the woods. I crossed the lawn and found a tree to sit under. Then I leaned back against the trunk and stared up through the bare branches at the blue sky, just letting my mind drift.

When I looked down again, I saw someone walking toward me from the building. I couldn't see his face, but there was something familiar about the way he moved. I knew who it was.

Angelo stopped a few feet away and stood with his hands in his pockets.

"I heard what you said in there," he said.

"I'm sorry . . . about all of it," I mumbled, tearing off a dry stalk and breaking it in half.

"You don't have to apologize. You just did, in front of all those people."

I threw the dry grass away and stared at the ground. "I really made a fool of myself, didn't I?"

"Yeah." Angelo smiled as I looked up at him. "You did."

He kicked an acorn sideways with his foot like it was a soccer ball.

"Beth Ellen took third place in her category. We're going out for ice cream to celebrate. Want to come?"

I squinted up at Angelo. "You want me to . . . after all I've done to you?"

Angelo stared off into the distance for a long time; then he looked back at me. He was frowning, and for a second I thought he might say, "No, actually, I don't." Then he shrugged. "It's a come-as-you-are party, Tucker."

I shook my head and smiled. Then I boosted myself off the ground and brushed the leaves off my pants.

"But I'm not eating any of that frozen yogurt stuff," Angelo said as we walked back toward the building. He gave me a play shove on the shoulder, knocking me off balance. "So don't go getting any ideas."

I tried to get him back, but he danced out of the way and ran backward up the walk ahead of me. He dodged every time I took a shot at him, so not a single swing hit the mark. Angelo Pighetti, the Michelangelo of spaghetti sauce and stage fighting. Angelo, my friend.

"Yeah," I said. "No more ideas."

CHAPTER 24

As it turned out, I was glad I wasn't going to Boston, because it meant I could have Thanksgiving with the Pighettis. They had a big party at the restaurant every year and fed everyone who walked through the front door whether they could pay or not. It was a real Italian Thanksgiving, with not only turkey and dressing but ravioli, spaghetti, lasagna, and of course, pizza.

My mom invited several of her patients. Mr. Kleinkopf was there and so was Louie, who passed on the turkey; the Sanchez family and Officer Venuti and his new girlfriend, Gina. I invited Mr. Wong, Ms. Bodine and Mrs. Hrabik. And Pig invited Beth Ellen, who showed up wearing a T-shirt that said: "The purpose of life is to create compost. The purpose of compost is to create life."

When everyone sat down to dinner, my mom gave the toast. "To friends," she said, raising her glass of Mrs. Pighetti's homemade Chianti in the air, "and to family, wherever you find them."

"Buon appetito," Angelo said.

"God bless America," Mr. Kleinkopf said.

"Feliz Navidad," Mrs. Sanchez added, carried away by the spirit of things.

"Oh well," Beth Ellen said. "It's the thought that counts."

It's spring now and school's almost over. My dad said I don't have to go to the Math and Science Academy unless I want to. Right now, I don't. But who knows how I'll feel when I'm older?

We still don't understand each other all the time, but at least we're starting to listen. Sometimes I think we're like the Sanchez family and the Pighettis. We can still care about each other, even if we don't speak the same language.

Angelo and I are going to work on the Pighettis' garden this summer, with some help from Beth Ellen and her award-winning worms.

We're also thinking of going out for the wrestling team when we get to high school, just in case Jonah's still there. I don't think we're going to be in the same weight class, but then you never know. I'm finally starting to get that growth spurt. And Angelo's actually lost a few pounds since Beth Ellen convinced him to become a vegetarian and take tai chi with her.

What he wouldn't do for science, he finally did for love.